PARADIGM AND OTHER SHORT STORIES

PARADIGM AND OTHER SHORT STORIES

E.P. HUBBS

Dalygood Media, LLC

For Megan

CONTENTS

Ghosts in the Sky

Ghosts in the Sky

From orbit, Naval Station Norfolk's complex looked like another uniform cell in the cement lifeform that had spread across the surface of Earth. Upon getting closer, insignificant aircraft could be seen floating from the airstrips like white paramecia swimming through the Virginian atmosphere. Within the labyrinth of corridors of the naval base was a small office with "Captain Patrick T. Nicholson" engraved on a sign hanging outside its door. Inside, a young pilot named James "Paladin" Odell stood at attention with his arms straight at his sides. His shoulders broadly pulled his uniform taut across his chest.

"I know what I saw, sir," he said firmly. He had short blonde hair and stood a good five inches taller than his portly superior standing in front of him.

The burly captain scowled at him and said, "And it was in your report, Lieutenant, where you should have left it. The Navy thanks you for your diligence, but you are not authorized to be spreading this shit around the base. This has the highest level confidentiality and you're sending it through email-"

"I've been writing these reports for two years, sir. I've reported them. Marigold has, Blitz and Oracle have too. Why isn't the Navy doing anything about them? These objects create a serious threat to us and our country. We feel-"

"You aren't here to lay bare your feelings, Lieutenant. I am not your therapist. You're here to fly where I want you to fly, and shut up when I tell you to shut up." The bald man struck the flint of his silver lighter and rolled the tip of a freshly cut cigar through the flame.

This is bullshit, Captain," Odell said while a bead of sweat ran from his temple. "If these were Russian planes, we wouldn't be ignoring them."

"That's enough, Odell," the Captain said loudly. He furrowed his wiry gray eyebrows. "Get back to your quarters. You've got an early flight tomorrow."

"Sir-" the young Lieutenant started.

"Not another word or I'm grounding your ass for a month. Dismissed."

Odell shot the seasoned Captain a rebellious smirk before turning to leave the office. He entered his quarters and a woman was sitting at the desk waiting for him. She wore a white tank-top, Navy-issued blue pants and black boots. Her reddish hair was pulled back; the tie struggling to hold the curls at bay. Her green eyes lit up as she saw him, and her bright smile contrasted against her dark skin.

She jumped to her feet. "You crazy son-of-a-bitch. Are you trying to make me find another wingman?" she said.

"Relax Blitz, you're still stuck with me. The old man just gave me a scolding," he said as he slapped his arm over her shoulder.

She brushed it off and crossed her arms. "The captain wouldn't escalate it?"

He laughed and replied, "Hell no. He told me to keep my mouth shut about them again. I can't be quiet any longer. People need to investigate these things, find out who made 'em, what makes 'em perform the way they do."

"It's definitely not natural. They give me the creeps," she said.

"I can't stop thinking about them. After watching them stay just out of our reach. It's like they're toying with us," he said weakly while rubbing his head.

"They have to be dangerous. Why would anyone build a craft like that without considering its capabilities in combat?"

Two more Navy personnel entered the room. Odell turned to face them and called out, "Well if it isn't our hard-working Wizzos. Where have y'all been?"

"That southern drawl never ceases to brighten my day, Paladin. I didn't think I was going to see you again," said Odell's Weapons System Officer, a tall Puerto Rican man who had been sitting behind Odell for the last two years. His call sign was "Oracle" as he always seemed to know the movements of enemy planes before they happened. He slapped hands with his flight mate.

"I'm glad you're still here," said the last member of the squad, the short blonde woman they called "Marigold" who was the WSO that sat behind Blitz, "I'm sure they only kept you around because of how expensive you'd be to replace."

Paladin smirked and said, "I'm thinking it's because of my impeccable flight record and unbeatable attack patterns, personally."

"You're not that good, flyboy. Blitz can fly circles around you without breakin' a sweat," she said while winking at her pilot.

"Aw, bestie,' the redhead said and the girls embraced each other.

"Yeah, yeah, enough of that," Paladin said. "It was still a failure. The captain said we can't even acknowledge the objects to anyone outside of official reports. He's sitting on his hands."

The four of them looked grim. Oracle spoke, "How can he do that? He has to know these things could take us out whenever they felt like it. I hate sharing the sky with them."

"It means he's already been told what to do with these reports by someone higher up," Marigold said. "He's been given orders to silence anyone who speaks up about them."

"Does that mean they aren't a threat?" Blitz asked. "Does he know they are friendly aircraft and we just aren't privy to it?"

Paladin shook his head. "Doubt it. You've seen them, they're too advanced. If an ally had this technology, we, being the most advanced military in the world, would have it too. And if it was Navy tech, we'd be the ones doing the test flights."

"Not much we can do about it. We'll have to take matters into our own hands," Blitz said.

"You mean-" Oracle started.

Paladin stepped toward him and said, "My friend already gave me the program. Once I install it we can record the flight data ourselves and give it to people who won't ignore it. If we don't act soon and they are a...foreign adversary-"

"You mean aliens," Marigold said.

"If they are aliens," Paladin continued, "and we don't do something soon, we'll be at an even bigger disadvantage should they decide to attack."

Blitz laughed and said, "They aren't aliens, you clowns. They're built by humans. New drone tech that we don't know about."

The four of them stood in silent contemplation for several moments.

Oracle cleared his throat and said, "Whatever they are, you're planning on leaking classified military intelligence. Don't you know what will happen to you?"

"Yes, there is a risk it will come back to me, but it will help us study them. It could save countless lives should they – whoever or whatever they are – attack. I'm not asking you to help me capture the data. I'm just asking you to watch my back while I do it."

The three of them nodded in agreement.

"Hell yes," Paladin said in a relieved exhale. "I'd rather have y'all up there with me than anyone else, alright? We fly with angel wings."

The four of them extended their arms and slammed their fists together in the center.

Blitz said, "Come on guys, let's play some pool."

Paladin stretched and said, "I'll pass. Tomorrow we're flying with weapons. I'm gonna try to get some sleep."

"Cutthroat it is, then," Oracle said. "The man needs his beauty sleep."

Oracle and Blitz walked out of the shared quarters but Marigold walked up to Paladin.

"Sorry, this is bothering me." She raised her small hand up to his head, then ran her fingers across his ruffled blonde hair to smooth it back into place.

"Uh, thanks," Paladin said.

She lowered her arm, looked into his blue eyes with her own and said, "Any time LT." She smiled before walking to catch the others on their way to the game room on another deck. Lieutenant Odell rolled into his bottom bunk and couldn't stop the grin from spreading across his face.

The airspace around Virginia Beach screamed with the booming sounds of Super Hornets shredding through the crisp morning air. The wide blue sky was streaked with white exhaust trails in pairs of two, two lead pilots with their wingmen riding with them. Paladin and Oracle flew one of the Hornets, Blitz and Marigold followed in the other, staggered to the right and about a hundred feet behind them. Over the radio, the familiar call came as it did on nearly a daily basis for the pilots.

"Scimitar One, Scimitar Two, we are seeing an aircraft on radar two miles south of your position, copy?"

Paladin replied sternly, "This is Scimitar One," he replied, "Copy that, Sanctuary. We'll try to get a closer look."

He slammed the flight stick to the left for an instant, spinning the plane ninety degrees, then tilted the stick toward him as the compass on his heads up display spun to the "S". He slammed the stick to the right, flattening the craft along the horizon, then pushed the throttle forward as the twin engines at the tail of the jet roared fire and shook their bones. Blaze hadn't missed a beat and mirrored the maneuver perfectly. She pulled up along Paladin's left as they sped past six hundred miles per hour.

"Alright buddy. Try to lock it in," Paladin said over his shoulder.

"Copy," Oracle replied. "Radar shows it. Rotate left two degrees to intercept. Altitude is Angels two-five. It's...hovering in the air. Completely still. Scratch that! Object just accelerated extremely rapidly, now traveling...three thousand miles per hour. Repeat, three thousand, and climbing."

Marigold's soft, intelligent voice came into their headsets, "How the...that's not possible. Thing just pulled over a hundred G's. No way."

"It's definitely one of them," Blitz said. "We would've heard anything else crash through the sound barrier. These things slice through it like warm butter...somehow."

Marigold said, "Should have visual confirmation in about twenty seconds. Vector is due southwest. We'll try to get it on the scopes. Maintain altitude," she said.

"Copy," Paladin said. He cycled through screens on the navigation display. He hesitated for a moment, then selected and opened a program he installed into the operating system secretly during pre-flight. The program loaded for a few seconds, then began recording data from the in-flight instrumentation as well as radio communications.

A glint of light flashed from somewhere to their left, catching Paladin's attention. When he looked over, he saw it. Flying at their side was a dark gray pyramid, elongated on the corner that was its nose, pointing sharply toward its destination. It was about the same size as his aircraft, but had no wings. As he studied it, his heart started racing and it became harder to breathe. He felt incompetent, weak, and pathetic. He couldn't believe someone could have technology so much better than them and they did nothing about it. He felt the fear spread through his body as he gasped for air.

"Got it on the scope," exclaimed Marigold. "Tracking it now. Damn, I can see it perfectly! You seeing this?" She stared at the grainy video feed on the monitor as the craft sped above the 3D terrain.

Oracle responded, "I see it. Looks like it's in a slight roll. The craft has no wings or visible engines. No exhaust of any kind detected. No temperature variance around the craft."

Marigold exhaled and said, "We haven't seen one spinning like this before have we?"

"Nope," Blitz said, "Sanctuary, should we engage the target? Now's our only shot – it'll outrun us right away after it crosses our vector."

"Negative, Scimitar Two, just watch it go. Do not engage, copy?"

"Copy that," Blitz replied.

Suddenly the craft veered straight toward the jets.

"Christ," Oracle said, "it's changed course, headed straight for us. Collision is imminent, ascend to angel thirty."

Paladin and Blitz pulled back on their flight sticks and climbed at a forty-five degree angle toward thirty-thousand feet.

"It's coming up too," Marigold said. "Sanctuary, bogey has engaged us and is approaching rapidly. Can we engage?"

"Negative, we have no intelligence suggesting the craft is hostile. We're tracking and will update you if the parameters of the mission change."

"No intelligence is right," Paladin said and shook his head. "This thing better not hit us."

"It's slowing down," Oracle said. "It's spiraling...and pulling up next to us."

Paladin looked to the right and saw the object rise into his field of view. It slowed considerably and sailed alongside them, matching their speed perfectly. The pyramid floated along their side as if it was studying them. It didn't look hostile, but more curious about their presence. They could see it making slight rolls as it cut through the sky.

"Um, what is this thing doing?" Paladin said with panic in his voice. "One has never willingly come close to us. They always just fucking disappear when we get anywhere near it."

The rolls slowly started changing form, with the craft making wider and wider circles in its trajectory. Then it shuddered suddenly as if it was experiencing the resistance of the air. It weaved and faltered, then tumbled end-over-end through the sky in a low arch toward the ground. Paladin pitched his Hornet back and forth slightly, a signal to his wingman to change to their private comms channel.

"Holy shit," Paladin said as he dipped the aircraft's nose down to chase the craft. "It's going to crash."

Marigold said, "Looks like some kind of malfunction. I see smoke coming off of it!"

Oracle replied, "It's going down. Watching for a pilot eject."

The craft plummeted lower and lower in an increasingly chaotic ballet. There wasn't an ejection. The craft struck the ground halfway up a hill in the vast green Virginian forest. There was no explosion or fire when it crashed. Instead, a plume of dust kicked up above the treetops upon impact.

"Listen up," Paladin said, "We cannot report this. I'm going to mark where it crashed and that's it."

"You're gonna go down there? You can't be serious, Jim. Naval intelligence needs this wreckage," Oracle protested.

"I have to know what this thing is. Every time I'm up here and I see one of them, I feel like it changes me. Like I can't think about anything else. And y'know what? I don't care about anything else. If the Navy won't tell me what they are, then I have to find out for myself. After I find out what it is, I'll hand it over to the Navy."

"I won't let you throw your career away over this," Oracle said firmly.

"Please Robbie. Don't tell them."

Oracle sighed over the mic, acquiescing. "Alright. I must admit, I'm curious myself. But for the record, you acted alone. We gotta switch back or they're gonna get suspicious."

Paladin switched back to the operation's radio channel and heard, "Scimitars, do you have visibility? Copy? Over."

"Acknowledged Sanctuary," he replied, "Negative visibility. Bogey just dropped off the face of the Earth. It disappeared, just like the others. Nothing on radar. It's a ghost, over."

"We aren't seeing it either," Sanctuary said. "Come on back home, Scimitars."

A few days later they were granted leave to go off base. Officially, they were going on a team-bonding camping trip into the hills. After sundown, the four of them rode together in a blacked-out military SUV. Blitz rode shotgun with her boots up on the dash and her phone plugged into the car speakers. They rolled down the twisting highway in silence for a half hour before "Grapevine Fires" by Death Cab for Cutie played. Oracle spoke up.

"Why do you have to always play this sad boy shit?" he said.

"It isn't shit," she defended without turning to face him. "Ben Gibbard can get it."

Marigold giggled. Oracle scoffed and said, "Girl, you are in the wrong profession. You want some man at home raising a kid while you're off fighting a war or what?"

"Maybe, but without the kid."

"So edgy. Next time I'm choosing the music."

"Yeah? I don't think anyone wants to listen to Ricky Martin."

"Just cuz he's Puerto Rican you think I listen to him? Get real, chica."

Blitz turned around and looked into his dark eyes. She saw his bright smile spread across his face. "Aren't you supposed to be navigating?" she said and turned to scroll on her phone again.

Oracle cleared his throat and accepted defeat. "I think the turn is coming up. Maps showed a dirt road here that'll get us close," he said.

"I hope no one has found it," Marigold said. "This is so exciting," she squeaked through her smile.

Paladin steered the SUV down the dirt road cautiously in silence.

Blitz caught herself biting her thumb. She quickly pulled it away from her mouth and said, "What the hell are we gonna find out there?"

"Answers," Paladin said and lowered his brow. "They've been a long time comin'."

They drove five more miles down the dirt road when Oracle had them pull off the road. They continued driving into the woods for a few hundred feet before parking the SUV so it couldn't be seen from the road. All four of them were dressed in black military fatigues with patrol caps and carried full backpacks with flashlights in hand. Blitz carried rope, Marigold an ax, and Oracle hauled a shovel. Paladin had a black bushmaster rifle slung over his shoulder.

The pilots instinctively mimicked their flying formation as they crept through the brush. Paladin led the way with Oracle following. Blitz and Marigold watched the rear and walked a few yards behind. With each step, the foliage grew brighter as a bluish light washed over the dark trees. They noticed faint patterns in the light that ran in long veins up the tree's bark and snaked across the damp green earth.

"What is that?" Blitz bent down and ran her hand across the blue patterns running through the dirt. "It almost looks alive, but...are these symbols? It's almost like code."

She watched as one of the light streams moved through her finger. She could feel it slowly moving the dirt from the ground into her skin like a flowing river. It felt like a flame was being held to her finger. She suddenly pulled back her hand from the pain and held it to her face. She could see the dirt had been pushed into her skin and wouldn't rub off. She could feel the dirt wasn't on the surface, but was actually *inside* her finger.

"What the hell?" she said as she held her swollen finger. "That really hurt! Don't touch it, Goldie."

Marigold crouched beside her and said, "Don't touch the creepy alien language imprinted on the ground? That's lesson one, chief."

"It's not just imprinted on it. The ground is moving, being physically manipulated by it somehow."

"Like they are one and the same," Marigold said as the two of them locked eyes.

"There's more of them," Blitz said, motioning towards the light. They stood and briskly caught up to the boys.

The four of them reached the edge of a small clearing, with felled trees forming a circular pattern from the impact point. The brilliant night sky was filled with stars that shone clearly without the lights of the city veiling them. The blue light they were tracking reflected brightest from the center of the crater. Within the aura of light, they saw the craft. It wasn't recognizable as a pyramid any longer; the impact broke it apart. Paladin climbed into the crater to get a closer look. The pieces were still tethered together by a material similar to a sheer plastic sheet. The blue lines of code streamed across the plastic surfaces and spread outward in all directions, shining brightly as they crawled up the walls of the crater.

Suddenly, the sounds of scraping metal came from the wreckage as the object shuddered. One of the pieces inched closer to another, pulled by the connecting sheet.

"I think it's repairing itself," Paladin called out over his shoulder. "Let's see if we can lift this thing outta here, c'mon."

The four of them surrounded the largest piece of the object, bent down, and dug their fingers underneath the strange, smooth, metallic pieces. They strained with all of their strength, but the machine didn't budge.

Oracle had his hands on his knees and spoke between breaths, "Maybe one of the smaller pieces, like this corner?" He pointed at one of the corner pieces that was about two feet across.

Paladin nodded and they circled it before bending down to lift the broken piece of metal. Unlike the main wreckage, the corner came loose and they held it there, but they couldn't fully tear it away from the sheet connecting it to the larger portion. They set it back down and caught their breath.

"It must be at least two hundred pounds," Oracle said.

"If we want to leave with any of it, I think that's our best bet. We gotta cut this plastic shit off and haul it back," Paladin said. "Goldie, gimme your ax."

Marigold held out the fire ax and Paladin took it. He approached the corner, raised the ax over his head, and slammed it down on the shimmering sheet as hard as he could. The sheet split down the middle but it wasn't a clean sever. Suddenly the object emitted a mechanical chirp so loudly and unexpectedly that Paladin fell to the ground, backpedaling away from it in a panic. The others dropped to a crouch and leapt a few feet away from the object, cupping their palms over their ears. The blue lights turned to a deep orange light that flashed several times a second. They stood around the machine, ready for anything, but the object made no more sounds. It slowly faded from the dark orange back to the bright blue hue.

Paladin walked up to it again with his ax at the ready. He peered over it to assess the damage. There was a five inch tear in the material which was glowing orange. He watched as tiny threads of orange light danced and wove themselves together along the wound, slowly repairing the damage. He shook his head and brought the ax down again in the same spot. It tore further, and this time the craft did not call out in pain. He brought the ax up and swung it down. Yelling out, he brought it up again, and down, over and over again as he screamed in rage.

He stood and caught his breath. "Benny," he yelled, "Help me cut it! Come on!"

Oracle leapt toward him to the opposite side of the sheet and cut at it with his shovel, alternating the swings with his co-pilot.

Having no cutting tools of their own, the girls watched them swing with everything they had as blow after blow damaged the connector further. Finally, the sheet snapped from the corner piece and curled against the core, causing another deafening chirp to echo through the pitch-black forest. In the vast canvas of the night sky above, a web of lightning cracked across the looming clouds and the crashing thunder answered back.

"Come on!" Paladin yelled at them, "We gotta get this thing out of here!"

They all scrambled around the severed corner and frantically grasped at the cool surface. Raindrops started falling around them, pinging against the strange metal. They pulled and pushed its deceptively heavy weight away from the core, up the side of the crater, down the slope and into the forest. Their ears were ringing from the chirp, but they could hear their hearts pounding as they went. They panicked as they slipped across the wet rocks; pushing forward any way they could until they finally reached the vehicle. They heaved it into the bed of the SUV and the rear suspension lowered to the back tires.

"We got it," cried Paladin as he slammed the rear gate shut. "Let's go!" he called through the drenching rainfall. As he walked back to the driver door the lightning flashed brightly, revealing one of the pyramid objects floating ahead of him for an instant. Its sharp nose was pointing directly towards him, then was consumed into the darkness. It made no sound and hid in the pitch black, but Paladin could hear the rain hitting the metallic surface a few yards ahead.

"Shit, they're onto us!" Oracle shouted.

He shouldered his rifle and aimed toward the object. The darkness howled with gunfire as he emptied fifteen rounds in quick succession. He stopped for a moment and another flash of lighting filled the forest, revealing the haunting trees that looked like fingers closing them in their grasp. Empty space being pierced by raindrops was the only thing that remained where the craft once floated.

"It's gone!" Paladin screamed. "Everyone get in!"

They piled into the SUV. Paladin floored it through the forest, barely dodging the bigger trees and driving straight over the small ones. They skidded onto the dirt road and started picking up more speed. Marigold rolled her window down and stuck her head out as if she was about to throw up. The cool air felt good as it whipped her long hair freely out of the window. She caught her breath and turned her eyes to the sky. Several gray pyramids noiselessly slid through the air overhead, flying past them and towards the crash site.

She brought her head inside and rolled up the window. "I just saw more bogeys. They crossed overhead. It didn't look like they were pursuing us."

"That's good considering that you shot at them!" Blitz said from the passenger seat and punched Paladin in the arm.

"I hit nothing but air! You still don't think they're aliens? Holy shit," Paladin said.

Blitz held her head in her hands, her red curls bouncing across her wrists from the bumps in the road. Marigold put her hand on Blitz's shoulder. She lifted her head and turned around to look at Marigold.

"What the fuck was that?" Her green eyes welled with tears. "What have we done?"

Paladin answered, "We can't know right now....but we're gonna find out. It's only an hour or so to Mack."

"That's your hacker friend?" Oracle said.

Paladin nodded.

They drove for miles along the forest highway without speaking before finally pulling onto a dirt driveway and parking in front of a large brown A-frame house. It was a secluded mountain retreat, surrounded by miles of forest on all sides. A bald man burst out of the squeaky front screen door, ran across the deck, and down the stairs towards them.

"Did you get it?" he called out while trying to keep his bathrobe closed.

Paladin opened the rear tailgate of the SUV and gestured his hands towards their prize. Blue lines of code sprouted from it since they last saw it along the vehicle bed it sat upon. The car interior had changed and the tendrils of code slithered up the walls across the glass windows.

Mack started yelling and dancing around in celebration and said, "James, I can't believe you've done it! You have succeeded admirably, my friend. Here she is!" He quickly pushed his square framed glasses up the bridge of his nose and focused on the anomalous technological wonder before him.

"What are these things? Is it attached to the car in some way now?" he asked.

"They kind of...retract when we move it," Marigold said, "We should be able to lift it out."

"Very well, let's get it into my workshop," Mack said.

They all lifted the craft, which seemed heavier even with the extra pair of hands, and waddled across the yard to a large building with sheet metal walls. They took it inside and placed it on a wide oak table in the middle of the room. As they sat and caught their breath, the small tendrils of code dripped off of it and slithered through the surface of the table. The blue lines moved slowly as they went, navigating the surfaces like the roots of a plant.

"We think it's trying to repair itself," Blitz said. "It's reaching out and clinging to objects around it to draw power from them."

Mack nodded. "Power, or matter. That's quite a trick to build machinery from wood. Absolutely captivating," he said while tapping a pen to his lips. "I'll have to run some tests. Here is the number to a burner phone I have. It's too risky for me to contact you at the base. Check back with me in a few days." He handed Paladin a small piece of paper with the number on it.

"Thanks for doing this, Mack," Paladin said.

"You have allowed me exclusive access to the greatest scientific discovery in the history of the Earth. My friend, thank *you*," Mack said with a smile. They shook hands.

The pilots piled into the SUV and drove back to their quarters at Naval Station Norfolk. They didn't speak for the entire trip, nor when they crawled into their beds and pretended to sleep.

The next morning two men entered their quarters and forcibly pulled Paladin out of bed, walking him straight to the Captain's office in his underwear. He stood at attention in front of the commanding officer.

"You want to explain yourself?" the Captain said while glaring at him.

"In regard to what, sir? I haven't sent any more emails," Paladin said while squinting to ease the sudden brightness of the red sunrise through the window.

Captain Nicholson walked over to him and held a flash drive in front of his face. "Explain to me, Lieutenant, why you installed software into your Hornet. Software designed to steal data from the United States Navy?"

Paladin's face flushed with red.

"You're lookin' mighty guilty there son." The Captain looked past him and called to the two men outside. "Get him outta here. Take him to the holding cells where he can rot until we decide when to have a trial."

Paladin looked at him with pleading eyes, but didn't know what to say.

The old man's face seemed to sag even lower and he shook his head. "You disgust me, Odell. You're no longer a member of the Naval Forces. Good riddance."

Odell's face soured as the two officers grabbed his shoulders and dragged him down the hallway away from his friends. The Captain marched down the hallway to the pilot's shared quarters with a few other Navy personnel.

He entered and spoke loudly, "Pilots, get up and fall in line."

The three remaining pilots jumped out of bed and stood at attention. On the desk behind them, the small piece of paper that Mack had written his phone number was in plain sight.

"Odell has been arrested for treason against the Navy," The Captain explained. "He was trying to steal and smuggle sensitive data off this base. We're trying to decrypt what was stolen."

He walked over to Oracle and pointed his finger in his face, "You flew with the traitor, Alvarez. You must have known about this. You're grounded until further notice."

"I don't know what you're talking about sir. Whatever he did, he acted alone," he said while looking straight ahead.

Blitz reached her arm behind her back and felt the surface of the desk. She slid her fingertips across the smooth wood until she grazed the small piece of paper. She pinched it between two fingers and quickly buried it in her pants pocket.

The Captain glared at her, but didn't see her sleight-of-hand. He snapped his head back to Oracle, his neck skin struggling to keep up. "I'm going to believe that because of your record, but you better hope to God I don't find any evidence in here." He shot glances at the two women and said, "Get off the base while we search your quarters. You'll still fly in the exercise tomorrow; I want you back in the morning. Dismissed."

The three of them took the SUV, driving well outside the exit gates of Naval Station Norfolk before uttering a word.

"God damn it," Blitz said from the passenger seat. "How could he forget about the program?"

"I did too. That thing distracted us," Oracle said while gripping the steering wheel tightly. "Well, he's paying for it now."

"I feel so bad for him. He's worked his whole life to get where he was and now it's all been taken away," Marigold said meekly from the back seat.

"It's okay, Goldie, you can find another boyfriend," Blitz said half-jokingly.

"He was not my boyfriend!" Marigold said and turned red.

"It's these damn machines," Oracle said. "If he wasn't so obsessed with them, he'd still be with us. Who the hell am I supposed to fly with now?"

"Well we've come this far," Blitz said. "I'm calling Mack to see if he's found anything. Start heading that way, Robbie."

Oracle shook his head and sighed. Blitz keyed the number into her phone and the note disappeared into her curls.

"James?" Mack said.

"It's Tiffany – we met yesterday. Listen, James was arrested about an hour ago. The Navy found your program."

"If they have the data, they'll go to the crash site and find your tracks," Mack said. "It's only a matter of time until they know we took a piece. Not that it will matter for much longer."

"What do you mean?"

"It's been reconstructing itself since you brought it to me. I still don't know the mechanism that allows it to transmute matter, but I've documented it at least."

Blitz shot worried glances at her friends and replied, "You think it's close to being functional again? Can you stop it?"

"It's about three fourths complete. No way of slowing it down either. I suspended it off the ground, but it absorbed my damn engine hoist. We may not want to be here when it boots up."

"Do you know what its goal is? Who created it?"

"Yes. At least, I have enough to construct a convincing theory, which is the best we can ever hope for, right?"

"I'm putting you on speaker. It's just us in the car, no one else."

"Hello friends. So my thinking is that this thing is from elsewhere. Created by things that are not human. Not from Earth."

The three of them exchanged concerned glances.

"Paladin was right," Marigold said.

"Yes he was," Mack said, "I let it connect to my laptop and the connectors forged a communication between the two. I was able to interface with it and access its infrastructure. It's coded in a completely unique language, unlike anything in our history of linguistics and computer science. The way it stores and transfers data is in line with how physicists predict quantum computing will function, once it's been invented of course."

"So you hacked into a flying alien computer?" Marigold asked.

"It's not just a computer – it's a quantum computer, far beyond our current technology. Studying this tech will leap us ahead hundreds of years."

"That doesn't prove it's built by aliens. Some genius somewhere could've made a breakthrough that changed the game," Marigold said.

"Let me continue," Mack said. "My laptop was able to find a signal within the code. More specifically, an interstellar transmission, sending all of this data straight out into space. When I viewed the signal, it was footage. Footage of us, of you all flying together in the air. Footage of forests, birds, cars, cities, cats–everything and everything about our planet. Why would humans be doing this, and beaming it away from Earth?"

Oracle thought for a moment and said "So it's like a hyper-advanced space telescope?"

Mack replied, "It appears that way. Humans are curious, we want to know what's out in space, so we search for it. But even if we see a planet we think has life on it, we can't see what the lifeforms look like or how they live. They're just too far away. These pyramid objects have crossed the enormous gap of space and arrived here with no pilots. They are fully automated, AI-driven telescopes that fly around the surface of Earth and beam back recordings to their home world."

"Just like we will probably do someday," Oracle said.

"We already do this on Mars," Marigold said. "We first saw Mars through a telescope, then we landed some robots on it to take pictures."

Blitz ran her fingers across her scalp and said, "But for us, that's not enough. We've always been planning to go see Mars firsthand. To land people on it and colonize it."

"They probably have the same plan. Hell, they might even be here already," Oracle said.

Mack said, "Their tactics aren't necessarily aggressive. I haven't found any weaponry built into it yet." He paused and said, "Look, I've got more work to do. The clock is ticking. See you when you get here." He hung up.

A few hours later, the black SUV pulled up and parked outside Mack's workshop. Blue light spilled from the cracks between the sheet metal lining the outside of the shack. They quickly walked up to the door and swung it open. The blue pulsating tendrils had grown to cover the floor, walls, and ceiling, filling the room with the same bright blue light from the crash site. The object was almost fully reconstructed, with only a few chunks across its surface that hadn't been filled in with the cool, other-worldly metal.

Mack was laying on the ground and facing the pilots as they entered, weakly propping himself up with his arms to gaze at them. The tendrils had driven themselves into his legs and snaked across his entire body. His face was made of blue light flowing across his skin, with his eyes shining with white beams.

"Oh no. It got him," Blitz said as she cautiously approached him.

Mack's teeth were black and could barely be seen moving as he spoke with his familiar raspy voice, now intertwined with the crackling of electricity.

"I wanted to give my energy to it...I chose to...or maybe it reached out...took me...but it deserves me," Mack said between sluggish breaths. "I am at peace. My body will be used to further their purpose, for their purpose is...purer...truer...than all the trivial pursuits of humanity. They are superior to us, but we are also them. Do not fight, feeble-minded warriors. Have the intelligence to...submit."

The three of them stood in silence around the craft and the man who collapsed as the code drained his last gasp of life from him. With that, the tendrils of code retreated, sliding back into the core pyramid. In an instant, the craft floated from the ground and hovered a few yards off the ground. Oracle ran and leapt toward some big chains that were lying in the corner of the workshop, lifting them with his bear-like arms. He swung the hooked end over his head and launched it over top of the craft.

"Quick! Tie it down!" he shouted. As the girls moved towards the chain to help secure it, the craft shot straight upwards at blistering speed, destroying the roof and scattering pieces of it throughout the surrounding woods. Oracle's voice was heard for a split second as the craft broke through, pulling him through the hole in the ceiling. In the sky above, the inertia wrapped him in the chains and split him, launching his body far into the night sky before the chains themselves splintered over the craft and fell to the Earth.

Blitz sat on the edge of her bed, slumped over with her head between her knees. She knew she had to get dressed for the day's flight but hadn't been able to. Marigold walked out of the bathroom in her olive flight suit, the tears in her eyes magnifying her blue eyes. She walked over to Blitz and crouched in front of her.

"C'mon airman. We gotta get in gear," Marigold said with a shaking bottom lip. She reached out and placed her hand on the top of Blitz's curls. "I know it's tough, but we're still here. We can't be brought down too."

Blitz looked up at her and locked her emerald eyes onto Marigold's baby blues. They both nodded and smiled, and Blitz stood to put her flight suit on.

Blitz wiped a tear from her cheek and looked at the wet spot on the back of her hand. Within the dirt that had fused into her pointer finger, she saw faint shimmering blue sparkles of light. She raised her hand to her face to get a closer look.

"What's wrong?" Marigold asked.

"Nothing," Blitz said and pulled her glove firmly over her hand. "Let's get on with it."

A few hours later the girls were soaring over the Atlantic coastline of Cape Charles at ten thousand feet in their swift gray bird. Once again, Sanctuary had picked up an unidentified craft. This time it was three of them traveling together, twenty miles north of the lone Super Hornet.

Sanctuary talked calmly over the radio, "They're flying low, one thousand feet...in an echelon formation. Over."

"Copy that Sanctuary. Should we engage? Over." Blitz asked.

"Negative, Scimitar. You know not to engage any craft without a wingman. Keep your current course and report anything you see."

"Copy that," Blitz said. She turned off the radio and spoke over her shoulder to her partner. "We're going to take a closer look. Can you lock on to them?"

"If you say so," Marigold said and tuned her tracker for a few minutes. "Got 'em. They are heading east. They're going slow, we'll intercept in forty seconds after course correction."

Blitz glanced down at her flight stick and something caught her eye. She could see light shining out of the gap between her glove and the sleeve of her flight suit. She grabbed the sleeve with her left hand, keeping her right hand on the flight stick, and pulled it back. Her wrist and forearm were covered in shifting, slithering, bluish veins. She slid the sleeve back to cover it.

"Fuck," she said.

"What is it?" Marigold asked.

Blitz spoke with a shaky voice, "When I touched the light, I think something changed in me, Kate."

"Changed like how?" Marigold asked sternly.

Blitz ripped her glove off and raised her right hand to show her partner sitting behind her.

"Changed like I'm turning into one of them," Blitz said. Two tears ran down her cheeks from beneath her wide black visor.

"What the hell, Tiffany? What is that?" Marigold's voice choked with panic.

Blitz sheathed her hand again, gripped the stick, and threw the throttle forward. The engines launched the plane through the sky. She dipped the nose toward the ground and corkscrewed the plane forty five degrees, then leveled it out facing north.

"We can't engage them," Marigold yelled. "We have to get back to base and get you help!"

"I can't stand them, Goldie. They took everything from me. I'm going to kill them." Blitz said while baring her teeth.

"Tiff, no. If you do this it's over for both of us! Please, go back," she pleaded.

Tiffany "Blitz" Alexander flipped the red plastic safety cover free from the missile launch button on the top of the stick. She felt the pulsating veins of light coursing through her arm start to pull in plastic and electronics from the flight stick she gripped. The materials blended into her flesh, even the electricity itself flowed through her as she began to become one with her aircraft. She felt the power starting to fill her being, ascending her to something more than human.

The flight indicator lit with green squares around the three pyramids in front of them. The green square around the object in the center of the flight pattern turned red, indicating they were close enough for missile tracking. She positioned her finger above the missile fire button as her eyes began to glow in white light.

Her voice was filled with sadness and cracked with electricity as she said, "I'm sorry, Goldie. I love you." She clicked the button and a missile dropped off the wing and shot past their nose, forming a wide spiral toward its target.

"Damn it!" Goldie shouted as she gripped the black and yellow loop in between her legs and yanked it upwards. The cockpit cover above her head lurched upwards and her ejection seat followed it. The wind rushed furiously around her as she tumbled through the air, then the parachute deployed and jolted her into a slow drift. She watched as the missile approached the alien craft. She thought it was about to hit, but the craft reversed course and shot straight towards the missile too fast to see clearly. It flew straight through the missile which erupted in flames, but the craft kept flying, straight toward Blitz and through her Hornet, which erupted into a second explosion. The craft sped away, completely unfazed, and faded into the endless blue.

"No, Tiff. No," she murmured as she watched the aircraft wreckage falling towards the Earth out of the smoke plume. She frantically glanced around the sky but couldn't see any of the alien aircrafts. As she made the controlled descent in her ejection seat, she cried and watched the wreckage trickle across the dense forest.

Her ejection seat crashed to the ground loudly. She ripped off her seatbelt and bounded through the forest toward a billowing of black smoke rising over the treetops. Tree branches whipped at her face as she sprinted down into a gulch. She quickly found what she was looking for. Blitz was leaning against a piece of the metal craft. Her lower half was severed and charred from the explosion, but the blue tendrils spread from her in all directions.

Marigold skidded to a stop in front of her friend. "Tiff," she said between sobs.

Blitz looked at her with the white light streaming from her eyes. Her body flowed with the blue code, and light coiled along her curly hair. "Kate. It's okay," she said with electricity in her voice. "This is the best way. Trust me. It's the only way we can all fly together again. I can feel Robbie. He's out there, transformed just like me."

"Oracle is okay?" Kate said, wiping tears.

"Yes. They...chose us Kate. They thought we were worthy enough for this power."

"I don't want to change," Kate said, falling to her knees in front of her.

"We can do anything we want...and we can do it together. You have to take this gift for yourself... and give it to Paladin too."

"Give it to Paladin?" she responded quietly.

"Yes. It's the only way you can be with him now. Take my hand, Kate," she said as she pulled the tendrils extending from her right hand out of the ground and held it out towards her friend. "Take this power as your own, please. We need you."

Goldie hesitated for a moment, but outstretched her hand. When their fingertips touched, she felt the light flow from Tiff into her own body, through her hand and up her forearm. She screamed and pulled against Tiff's grip, digging her heels into the dirt. She was able to break free and fell onto her seat.

A smile filled with white light spread across Blitz's bright face. "Now go," she said. "Go free him. I'll see you in the clouds," She touched her hand to the ground again and the tendrils buried themselves into the Earth, expediting her transformation.

Goldie looked at her hand, now faintly glowing with blue light along the veins in her arm and her fingertips. She crawled to her feet, pulled her sleeve to her wrist and put her glove over her hand.

After the rescue helicopter picked Marigold up, she debriefed with the Captain. She explained that they were attacked by an unidentified aerial phenomenon and Blitz had failed to eject. He pressured her about how the rescue teams weren't able to find a crash site or any debris. She just shrugged and asked to rest.

On the way to the barracks, she slipped down the opposite hallway and went to the holding cells at the south end of the base instead. She talked her way past the guard on duty, telling him the Captain had sent her to tell Paladin the news about Blitz being shot down.

"The Captain wanted me to rub it in his face. It is the bastard's fault after all," she said.

The guard nodded in agreement and allowed her into the cells. She smiled slyly when out of his view, blue light flickering in her mouth. She rounded the corner and found Paladin's cell. He stood from his bed and ran towards the cell's bars, grabbing them in his hands.

"Goldie!" he shouted and couldn't hold back his smile. "What are you doing here?"

"I'm here to say goodbye. They're all gone, James," she said, holding back her tears.

"What do you mean?" he said as the color left his face.

"When we went back to Mack's, that thing killed Robbie. So we came back to base like nothing happened. Then Tiff and I flew today, and she attacked one of them. But we were outmatched...I ejected before she was taken out of the sky." Her voice shook as a tear rolled down her cheek.

"Shot down? They...they're gone?" he said in disbelief.

"The crafts were...superior. You should've seen how it moved. It was like...it knew it was unstoppable, and that we were just these fragile, insignificant, insects." She walked up and put her gloved hands over top of his hand. "And now, you're going to be stuck in a cell for who knows how long. Will you give me one last kiss...for old time's sake?"

He blushed and leaned forward. Their lips met in the gap between bars, and when her mouth opened, the light filled his, and he felt the energy surge through him. He pulled away and looked perplexed.

"What was that, Goldie?"

She smiled and light beamed out of her mouth. "I just saved you, James. Now we will become more powerful than we ever could before. We'll turn into them and be together forever."

He stared at her in disbelief. "You tricked me?" he asked.

"It was the only way we could be together, James. The only way we could fly again," she said and reached through the bars to fix his disheveled hair. "Promise me you'll join me among the stars."

James thought for a moment as he looked into her sparkling blue eyes and said, "Okay. I promise."

She smiled at him, then turned and walked out the door. He slowly stepped backwards until his back hit the concrete wall, and he slid down it to sit on the floor. In his mind, he felt something new. A small, warm presence, like a candle flame, flickering in the deepest reaches of his conscience. He closed his eyes and focused on it. He felt the distant presence of Blitz and Oracle, flying together at immense speed, chasing each other playfully through the atmosphere in their new forms. They felt completely free.

He was filled with joyous awe as their power grew within him. He felt a building anticipation for his new abilities. Reaching outward, he sensed more, not just his friends, but thousands of the objects. So many more, expanding in all directions away from Earth across the void of space and onto other worlds. He was overwhelmed by the enormous complexity of the feeling but knew that soon he would be able to fully comprehend it.

The door opened and Captain Nicholson strolled up to his cell bars.

"Odell. I got your court date set. It's only a few months away, lucky you. We'll have plenty of time to get to know one another better."

Odell stared at the floor, his blonde hair covering his eyes, and said, "Don't worry, sir. I won't be here."

"What the hell did you say?"

Odell lifted his head slowly and stared at the captain. A grin slowly spread across his face, and his smile beamed with bright white light.

Paradigm

Paradigm

Steph regretted wearing all black to her Zoom interview. She chose the outfit in an effort to stand out, but the cheap webcam made her dissolve into the dark fabric of her office chair, making her look like a floating white face. Her blonde hair was tied up in a ponytail which made the effect worse. She nervously watched the mic icon flash as it picked up the shrieks of her neighbor's children permeating through the frail walls of her apartment. She felt the box fan in her window blow across the small beads of perspiration forming on her neck.

"Dreams?" she clarified to the man patiently smiling at her on the screen.

"Yes. Do you ever have any lucid dreams, Steph?" His voice was deep and was distorted by her shaky connection speed. His picture kept blending into a pixelated mosaic, then sharpening again.

"I do. Not very often though. I think it's really fun when it happens."

"Do you have a favorite?"

"I can only think of one," she felt her face turn red as she decided if it would make her look bad or not. She hesitantly continued, "It's so cheesy, like one of those low-budget romance movies."

"I don't mind," he said and smiled.

"I was in New York City, I think. I'm walking across the park with a bunch of textbooks in my hands. I'm looking up at a huge marble archway and wham! Some guy walks into me! He helps me up and we lock eyes. That's the moment I knew it was a dream. It was one of those perfect romances that could only happen in a movie. So, I played the part."

"It sounds wonderful," he said. "Lucid dreaming is a rare quality, you know. Not everyone can do it." His eyes were hidden by the reflection of the screen in his glasses.

"Can I ask, what does that quality have to do with the job?"

"We'll get there eventually," he said. Clearing his throat, he shifted in his seat. "Now, the job specifically entails coding in virtual reality environments, which I see you have some experience in. We are also working with neural link interfacing, are you familiar with that tech?"

"You have...functioning neural links?" Steph asked. "Wiring the brain to communicate with an AI directly? I know that tech was being worked on, but I thought it was decades away from being usable."

Malcolm took his glasses off and stared into the camera. Upon seeing the gray color of his eyes, Steph felt something stir in her consciousness. He seemed familiar to her in some way. Looking into his eyes was oddly comforting. The video quality suddenly shifted and his eyes turned into distorted blocks on the screen.

His voice crackled through the speakers as he answered, "We have them working at high levels in a few of our employees. First, we studied the technology while attempting to cure neurological diseases like Parkinson's. Through these studies, we learned so much about electrical impulses in the brain and found that sending and receiving data signals was not so difficult."

"Any idea when they would hit the market?" she asked, trying to suppress the doubt in her voice.

"The timetable for release is one year from now, assuming our new programmer can sort out some of the quirks. That would be one caveat, if one could call it that, regarding the job." Malcolm said. "Steph, we would need you to get one implanted. It's the only way to interface with the system."

Steph's eyes widened. She stared at the bald man past concerned brows, trying to figure out if this whole thing was a joke. "You want to wire my brain?" she asked, her doubt showing through this time. "Tell me, do you have one implanted?"

"Yes, I've had one for about a year. Look, you're a programmer. Ask me a math question. Let me show you how useful this will be for you."

"Okay," she thought for a moment. "What is...4600 multiplied by 3253 squared?"

"Forty-eight billion, six hundred seventy-seven million, two hundred forty-one thousand, four hundred," he said quickly.

She tapped the equation into her phone calculator and confirmed the answer.

"Holy shit," she paused and suddenly felt light-headed.

"It's a lot of power we're talking about. Being paired with an AI—it's life-changing. In many ways." His eyes rapidly darted across her face as if he were analyzing her facial responses.

"I can only imagine," she said and glanced away from the screen to the grid of plastic string showing through a tear in the old brown carpet on her bedroom floor. She contemplated what it would feel like to have metal wires invading her brain tissue. She shivered and looked back at the screen.

Her speakers kept talking, "Listen, based on our conversation today, and your past experience, I think you'd be a great fit for the company. The salary is adequate to say the least. Will you work with us?"

"How adequate?" Steph asked.

"We'll start you out at two hundred thousand annually. But what you will learn working for us is worth far more than that. Trust me."

Steph watched her emerald eyes widen in her small on-screen portrait. She replied through a beaming smile, "Alright, sign me up."

The next day, Steph left behind her dingy apartment and took a car to the airport with a single suitcase. She had a brief conversation with her mother to tell her the news. Her mother doubted her decisions, like she always did, so Steph hung up on her. Leaving everything behind felt freeing. There was nothing left for her in Boston anymore. All her childhood friends had married and left the city. It had been almost a year since she left her ex, and she quit her job almost three months prior. She told herself she should have done this a long time ago. After five hours, she woke from her in-flight nap as she arrived at Denver International Airport. Her jaw dropped when she saw the red light of the morning sun brightening the looming faces of the Rocky Mountains for the first time.

A driver picked her up and drove her high into the coniferous mountains of Colorado. After several hours of winding through steep canyons on dirt roads, they passed a security gate with Singularity, Inc. signage posted on it. They continued for a few miles before arriving at an enormous concrete bunker built into the side of a mountain. She climbed out of the car and stared up at the granite sheets that towered over her. The remoteness of the area gave her an uneasy feeling.

She cautiously pushed the tall stone entrance doors open and walked into the complex. A large wooden reception desk was inside. A tall man wearing dark chocolate-colored velvet suit with a black tie and matching undershirt was leaning against it. She realized it was Malcolm, the man who had interviewed her.

His black dress shoes tapped on the stone floor as he approached her. "It's great to meet you in person, Steph. Welcome to Singularity," he said and shook her hand.

"This place is amazing, I've never seen mountains like these."

"Of course not, you're a New York girl," he replied.

She tilted her head and said, "Boston, actually. I've never lived in NYC."

"Oh, that's right. Your dream was in New York. My mistake," he said. "Let me show you around."

Through a nearby metal door was a garage filled with a few dozen cars. "You can take any of the company cars if you need a joyride. However, I'd suggest staying in and relaxing in one of our virtual environments instead. It's much safer," he said and closed the door.

They stepped into a shiny metal elevator and rode it down forty floors. Steph didn't know what to expect, but what opened before them looked like a luxury resort mixed with a military research facility. The corridor was immense, with cushy red carpet, intricate light fixtures hanging from the high ceilings, stained oak trim, and white painted walls. Clearly, Singularity didn't mind investing in aesthetics. She began to feel like she had made the right decision, though she was still nervous about getting machinery implanted in her brain.

She followed Malcolm down the corridor and noticed a woman with short, dark brown hair was walking toward them and wearing an odd-looking black hooded jumpsuit.

She smiled as she noticed Steph and called out, "Hey, new girl. I'm Samantha, the head neuroscientist. We'll be working closely together. I'll catch up with you when you're ready to get calibrated." She passed Steph with a wave and continued down the corridor. Steph waved back at her. As Samantha turned her head Steph noticed a small, square-shaped scar showing through her hair just behind her ear.

Malcolm led her through a doorway into a spacious room. There were couches and a coffee table surrounding a wall-mounted screen and a fireplace beneath it. On the opposite wall was a small kitchen with a man standing at the counter, and in the corner was a huge metal chair reclined like a hospital bed.

"This is your new room. I hope it's suitable. Let me know if you need any other accommodations." Malcolm motioned toward the couch. "Please, take a seat. Graham can get you a whiskey sour if you'd like. He is our concierge manager."

"It's a bit early for me to be day-drinking on the new job," she said with a laugh. "But how'd you know that was my favorite drink?" She turned back toward the man standing in the kitchen and said, "I'll take an orange juice, thank you Graham."

"Just a lucky guess. It's not too early for me. A sour for me please, Graham," Malcolm said with a smile.

"Coming right up," Graham said as he shook a drink tumbler.

"Now," Malcolm exhaled as he sat on the opposite couch, "I'm sure you have some questions."

"Yeah, I have a few."

Graham placed the drinks on the oblong wooden coffee table between them.

"For starters, what's with the chair?" Steph asked and took a drink of juice.

"It aids in capturing dreams. We call it a Buffer." Malcolm stood up and walked toward the strange chair. "We built it to analyze one's dreams and record them. Revisiting dreams would be invaluable to psychologists, or merely for entertainment. People could even sell their dream recordings to other people. You can imagine how valuable of a market this could be."

"Sure, if it actually works."

"Currently it is capable of recreating what happens to the dreamer as a virtual, explorable space. Come take a look."

Steph walked over to the chair. "Where does it hook up to the neural link?" she asked.

"It's all wireless, with plenty of power tucked under the hood. Once you have an implant, you just have to get close enough and the chair will connect to you. It relays what your brain is perceiving and creates the virtual environment based on those signals. It's an extension to the neural link with added processing power."

He walked around to the back of the chair and placed both hands on the shoulder cushions. "Brains are slow at processing things. They read inputs at sixty bits per second...far inferior to any modern processor. The implant funnels the signals to and from the brain, and, with the Buffer's help, it processes everything quickly, allowing dreams to be recorded with accuracy and clarity."

While this all sounded interesting, Steph felt a wave of anxiety at the thought of getting the implant. She tried to hide her quickened breaths as she spoke, "How long does the implant procedure take?"

He turned his head and pointed at a faint scar behind his left ear in the shape of a perfect square. "We just have to remove a small piece of skull to get in and connect everything, then we put it back. Samantha can do the procedure and you'll be healed up within a matter of days. Unlike me, you have plenty of hair to cover the scar," He smiled, reached his hand out as if he was about to touch her hair, but he brought his hand back to his drink and took a sip.

She locked eyes with him. She didn't know why, but she trusted him. Something about how attentive he was, and how unabashedly confident he was in every word he spoke. He was calm, gentle, and incredibly intelligent. She liked his sharply dressed, clean style, which was the opposite of her last relationship. 'He who shall not be named' was an unkempt underachiever who paid more attention to his fantasy football league than he ever did to her. The two that came before him were nothing but wasted years and embarrassing memories she wished she could forget. Malcolm, however, looked at her with a commanding interest that she had never experienced before. She wondered why anyone would give her such undivided attention.

She smiled at him, barely containing her excitement and said, "I'll do it. I want to get the implant."

Malcolm nodded at her and said, "That's wonderful, Steph. I also want to let you know that you shouldn't view me as your superior. I created this company, but you and Samantha have equal say in what decisions we make moving forward, no matter what we find. It's us three at the top. We'll be our own triumvirate. Sound good?"

"It does but...why would you give me that much stock in the company?" Steph asked.

"Personal philosophy. I don't think any one person should be in control of everything in an organization. It worked in Ancient Rome, didn't it?"

"For a while, yes," she said.

"Well, nothing lasts forever. At any rate, I have a good feeling about you," he said and walked toward the door.

He led her down the hallway to an operating room. The neurologist, Samantha, was there and a few nurses were working to prepare for the procedure.

"I'm so glad you've decided to join us," Samantha said to her.

Samantha had her lay on the hospital bed and the nurse put an IV into her arm. She had a sudden pang of regret, and thoughts that she made the wrong decision flooded her mind. She tried to protest but quickly lost consciousness.

She woke several hours later and sat up in the hospital bed. She reached behind her ear and felt a square patch covering the wound which she cautiously prodded with her finger. She slowly ran her finger across the buzzed-down hair around the wound. The sensations were otherworldly. She could feel each individual hair follicle as it moved and thought she could hear a faint crackling of electricity inside her head. Malcolm walked into the room and she quickly pulled her arm down.

"Morning," he said. "Everything went well, as expected. I told you, it's an easy procedure."

He walked over to the wall screen and an x-ray of her head popped up. She saw the familiar shape of a brain but running along each crease and fold was a network of small, white wires that extended from her brain stem like the trunk of a tree. They branched into endless smaller tributaries flowing all the way down to the smallest dendrites, making one interconnected electrical network of synaptic connections. The wires curled at the crest of her brain and connected to a row of six square processors. She tried to focus on the wires inside her head, to hear the electricity again, but couldn't feel anything.

"I wouldn't suggest testing it out yet. Control your thoughts. Don't let them run away from you. We'll start calibration tomorrow so get some rest," he said.

For three weeks, she stayed in various rooms doing warm up exercises to calibrate the implant to her brainwaves and thought patterns. Any memories she made after the implant could now be recalled in perfect clarity. She was able to quickly answer math problems and her vocabulary and reading speed tripled. She felt sharper, smarter, and more responsive in all of her daily activities, and found that she made mistakes less and less frequently. Learning new computer systems went incredibly fast as any mistakes were logged and avoided automatically by the assisting AI.

She interfaced with her phone and could make calls and speak to her mother without using her voice. Malcolm made her sign a non-disclosure agreement, so she couldn't reveal the true nature of her work to her mother or that she decided to become a cyborg. She didn't mind keeping it a secret. It was easy for her to do. With the assistance of the implant in her head, she found the conversations with her mother to be painfully slow and meaningless, like talking to a child.

Then Malcolm showed her the source code for Paradigm, the virtual reality program used to replay the recorded dreams. He suggested that she laid on the metal Buffer chair to boost her processing power and prevent any slowdown from the massive amounts of data. She did so and interfaced directly with the compiler. She visualized the code and explored it within her thoughts, interpreting and changing the code far more efficiently than ever before. As she scrolled through the thousands of lines of code, she felt her mind expand and branch into several different processes at once, allowing her to conceptualize every facet of the program.

After a few minutes, she exited the compiler, sat up, and looked over at Malcolm. While she was scouring code, Samantha had entered the room.

Samantha glanced down a checklist on her tablet and said, "That's all of the basic calibrations we have, Steph. We're ready to record one of your dreams, if you are."

"Does it matter what I dream about?" Steph asked nervously.

"Whatever you see will be recorded, even if you're too out of it to remember the dream."

Samantha walked over to Steph, holding a silver serving tray with a lone glass on it. It was half full of a clear liquid that looked like water. "This will knock you out completely and keep you in a dream state for as long as possible. Even if the connection isn't the strongest, Paradigm will record everything in the highest detail it can."

She took the glass and drank the cool liquid. Within four minutes, she was out cold.

She dreamt she was standing in the wilderness, surrounded by trees. Standing around her were fellow soldiers, strapped with armor and carrying weapons. The dream wasn't familiar to her and it wasn't lucid. She was completely unaware that she was in a dream. It felt real. Without question, she cried out for blood in unison with her fellow soldiers in a language she had never heard before. She ran forward through the lush forest, shoulder to shoulder with lines of lumbering soldiers. She glanced down to look at the weapon she was using. It looked like a silver rifle, but was completely alien in design. Yet, she pulled the full-hand trigger naturally, blasting blue energy shots that rushed through the air with electrified hisses out of the twisted barrel, arcing up the hillside toward the enemy and blowing them to pieces. She suddenly noticed that her arms were made of wood with dark brown bark growing all over them.

An explosion erupted from the ground in front of her, knocking her flat on her back. She felt the dirt stinging her "skin" and the warm spray of purple blood that coated her face. She rose to her feet in a burst of adrenaline and saw a foe charging over the hilltop, trampling over the corpses of her friends. She lost her weapon, so she charged bare-handed at the enemy who wielded a long spear-like weapon. When the soldier stabbed at her, she sidestepped and grabbed the spear, then wrestled it from his arms. Another explosion hit nearby and sent them both tumbling down the hill, the spear falling from her grasp. She sat up and crawled on top of the enemy soldier. She was able to pin his arms down with her knees, straddling him.

She screamed in the soldier's face and closed her hands around his neck, pushing downward as hard as she could. She noticed her hands didn't have fingers. Instead, she had two dull, black claws and a shorter one opposed them. She stared into the shiny black eyes of her enemy. His skin was blue and full of small cracks, like smooth rock that had split apart. None of this seemed odd to Steph. Everything felt normal as if she was really on this battlefield, even as a tear streamed down her face and she clenched her jaw muscles and grinded her teeth together. She gripped as hard as she could on this creature's throat and felt its windpipe collapse under her weight. She was sure it was dead when its eyes rolled back into its head. Then, she woke up.

She drearily gazed around the room for a minute before remembering where she was.

Samantha was standing by her side and said, "Easy Steph."

"Did it work?" Steph asked.

"Readings look good. Malcolm was linked up so he'll know for sure. He's on his way."

"He was watching me? God, I hope it wasn't something embarrassing," Steph said.

Samantha smiled and said, "Girl, you are blushing. Don't tell me you have a crush."

Steph dropped her jaw and was about to protest before Malcolm entered. He was out of breath and had a wide grin on his face, laughing as he buttoned his shirt. He walked toward her, arched over and clapping loudly.

"Well done, Steph. That was amazing," he exclaimed. He placed his hand on her shoulder.

"Wait, you saw it?" Steph asked groggily. "What was it? I can't remember. What was my dream?"

"I was watching it live," he said excitedly. "Let me show you the recording. After you've watched it, you'll remember it for good."

"Have fun, you two," Samantha said and winked at Steph.

Several rooms down from the dream room was a room labeled "Theater". Steph and Malcolm entered and stood in a spacious chamber with red padded floors and walls. They changed into Virtual Reality gear that was miles above the dinky plastic rig

Steph used at her last job. Instead of a visor, Steph pulled a thin hood over her blonde hair and stuffed the ends down around her neck. She realized why Samantha preferred a shorter hairstyle. The hood fit tightly around her face and only had an opening for breathing. Across the hole was a thin veil of fabric that Malcolm explained could seal itself to simulate suffocation, but not to worry because it had a safety built in to open again before it was too late.

The inside of the hood had an ultra-high-definition display in front of the eyes and surround sound speakers covered the ears. The suit she wore was made of the same material as the hood and could contract in response to the program—even creating pressure on the skin to simulate touch. Smells and taste—and some emotions—were recorded via neural link and could be recreated by sending those signals directly into the brain. Malcolm explained that the more and more integrated the software became with the neural link, the less necessary the suit would become.

"The goal is to get rid of this suit entirely, so we can experience all aspects of the simulation with only the neural link. That's what you'll be working with Samantha to accomplish," he clarified.

"I'm not fully sure what that means yet, but I'll learn it," she laughed. "Will we be in there together?"

"Yeah, we can walk around together in the virtual environment. Remember, this is just a digital recreation of your dream – we aren't going inside your head. Here we go."

The program booted to a white background initially, then changed to a blue sky. They stood atop an overgrown stone pillar with waterfalls cascading downward in a circle around them. The word "Paradigm" floated in the sky in gold cursive letters that sparkled in the artificial sunlight. Malcolm's virtual representation of himself looked just like his real-life self, and so did Steph's, but they were slightly less defined and detailed.

"It scanned your body and sculpted an avatar for you to use," Malcolm said and winked in a stuttered animation.

"Lovely. The graphics need to be tightened up in here a bit. I can work on that. How do you wink?" Steph asked.

"You just wink. The hood scans your face and reflects it in the simulation. Again, it would be better if this were relayed through the neural link and not the suit. See, it captures any movement," he said as his avatar leapt in the air and soundlessly clicked its heels.

Steph raised her arm and flipped Malcolm off. "Are you getting this?" she asked with a smile.

Malcom furrowed his brow. "Yes, thank you for that." He tapped his fingers on the menu that floated in front of him. "Enough tomfoolery. Loading it up."

Suddenly they were standing in a blurry forest of brown polygons. All the shapes started out simple and angular, then progressively rounded, gaining more and more complexity. The edges sharpened into higher definition and the forest took shape. Then, finer details began to spread across everything. The tree bark gained depth between each pixelated crack. The dirt changed from a smeared blob to millions of defined points. Then the flora popped in as thousands of blue ferns sprung from the ground. Grass swept across the dirt and moss across the tree bark. In a slowly building crescendo, the sounds of the forest crept in; she could hear flowing water in the distance and the chirping of birds and insects. The smell of the smoke and rain-drenched ferns were thick in the misty air. She felt the morning wind blowing softly across her skin, raising the hairs across it. Then the soldiers all loaded in at once, frozen mid-charge. Steph gasped and put her hands on her knees to steady herself from the disorienting motion. She remembered all of it now.

"These soldiers. I don't know how my mind could create them. I'm not a creative person," she said as she walked between the motionless warriors, marveling at the intricate engravings in the silver metal armor.

Malcolm laughed as he walked next to her. "I didn't take you for an expert in alien armor design. Which brings me to my next point – I think it's time we discuss the theory we have come up with. We call it – Dream Entanglement Theory."

"Fancy. What's the theory?"

He continued, "Samantha and I have visited thousands of dreams and can conclusively say that you didn't imagine these soldiers, Steph. They are real."

"You're saying I was really here?" she asked skeptically.

"Yes. What we see in our dreams is actually happening, just not to us. Each one is a glimpse into another universe. These events happened today, just not here on Earth."

"Where then?" Steph asked.

"On a planet trillions of lightyears away from us. Across the threshold of our observable universe, and many, many others; an unfathomably fast distance. We could never dream of reaching this place conventionally. And yet, here we are...seeing it with our own eyes."

Steph crossed her arms and said, "Why would I dream of this specific battle?"

"Are you familiar with quantum entanglement?" Malcom asked as he knelt and touched one of the strange, blue ferns.

"A little. I took some physics in college. Let's see," she tapped her lips in thought. "I think that's the concept that two atoms can become entangled on the quantum level."

"Which means if something interacts with that atom that same change can happen to the other atom at the exact same moment, even if they are light years away from each other," he said. "Crossing the vast seas of space instantaneously. Precisely."

She shook her head in astonishment and said, "So there's an invisible force that's always been there; a tunnel across space that we can access for a brief moment."

He stood and walked to one of the soldiers. "Have you ever noticed that you always perceive dreams from the viewpoint of looking through someone's eyes? In this case, it was this guy's perspective," he said, pointing to the motionless soldier standing in front of him. "You and he are quantumly entangled with one another...and countless others."

"He?" Steph asked as she walked around to the front of the alien. It was a male, based on the broad upper body and height. But his face, underneath the strange alien bark, was shaped like hers. She gazed straight into the same emerald eyes that she had seen in the mirror for her entire life. She stumbled back and almost tripped over a mossy log jutting out of the ground, but her feet passed through it without colliding.

"But...why is he different than me?" was the only question she could think of.

"In short, because the laws of physics are different here than in our own universe. Not much different. But during the Big Bang, there is an extremely narrow window of time where the expansion of the new universe occurs. It's called cosmic inflation."

"I remember that. That's when the forces governing our universe were decided. When elements and chemistry were made possible. Gravity and electromagnetism."

Malcolm smiled. "Exactly right. But this universe is not so different from ours." He ran his hand down the bark of a nearby tree. "Life still exists here. Plants. And these humanoids don't seem *that* different from us. Their strange skin could be the result of the slightest change during the inflation of this particular universe. Perhaps gravity's pull is slightly stronger here. Perhaps hydrogen weighs .0001% less than it does in our home universe. Or light travels faster, or more slowly. Each minute change means each universe forms with its own special quirks."

Steph glanced up at the sun. It was still the same blinding, white sun she had seen her whole life. She quickly looked away. "What happens if a change results in our solar system never spinning together, never forming planets? What if the sun was a blue giant? That version of Earth would be incinerated."

"We suspect this happens all the time, far more common than Earth forming and even closely resembling our home. But we'll never be able to see those universes. It seems we can only record journeys into other beings that formed extremely similarly to us. Beings whose molecules formed into the same basic shape as us, in the same basic way as we did. All of the other possibilities that stray too far from our genetic structure can't be visualized by us, so we simply don't dream about them."

"This is unbelievable," Steph said, noticing a network of strange blue vines that crawled down the tree trunks from the upper branches. "This version of Earth. These two warring factions. Human history never happened. Humans never happened."

"No, but something similar enough happened. Just some genetic differences, but the same carbon-based proteins all linked together in the same way that you are now. You and this being are linked on a quantum level across an unbelievably great distance."

The two stood for a while in silence as the weight of these notions bounced through their minds. Then, Malcolm asked, "Are you ready to watch the recording?"

"Yes," Steph replied as her perspective snapped from where she was standing into the eyes of her other self as her avatar disappeared. The sound of the strange weapon fire filled the air as the dream played out in the exact same way that she had dreamt it earlier.

Once the simulation was complete, Steph pulled her simulation mask off which was soaked in sweat. They both were standing in the Theater again. Malcolm embraced her as a fellow soldier and they cried out together, celebrating glorious triumph after their victory. She had never felt such exhilaration and was smiling so wide that her cheeks hurt. Reliving the dream with the neural link and virtual environment made it seem so much more real, especially after realizing it actually was a recording of something that *was* real. Her adrenaline dissipated and she felt ill. She walked over to the nearby couch and plopped down on it. Malcolm walked over and sat on the adjacent chair.

"Isn't it amazing?" He asked. "How does it feel to know that you are a killer?"

She glanced up at him and considered the question.

Malcolm laughed and said, "Don't worry. I am too. My journeys have taught me that anyone is capable of killing in the right circumstances. Samantha is too. I watched her beat in a robber's head with a frying pan. It was wild."

Steph shook her head in disbelief. "I guess people will do anything to survive. But knowing I could actually do that to someone...it's freaky," she replied. "How many of your dreams have you recorded?" She asked, trying to change the subject.

"I've recorded over nine hundred. Samantha is almost up to four hundred."

"Damn," she said. "Can I watch some of your favorites?"

Malcolm smiled and said, "Eager to see more, are we? I have plenty to show you."

Over the next few weeks, Steph watched dozens of Malcolm's dreams. Watching from his perspective was a constant exhilaration of new discoveries. She became obsessed with each new experience and watched as many as she could during the day. There was one where he was leaping high through the air and floating on command. That universe had some sort of anti-gravity suit they had invented which allowed freely controlled flight. The feeling of effortlessly floating through the air across the alien landscape was pure bliss. She viewed another dream where Malcolm was studying otherworldly plants in a giant indoor terrarium.

There was one where he was in an underwater race, riding atop a large seahorse-like creature. There was an unpleasant one where he was shot by a man stalking him through the alleyways of a city that she thought was New York. There was another where he stabbed a man to death with a plastic shank over a prison poker game. Another where he sat on the edge of a sky-scraper with his legs dangling over the edge while sending angry texts to a contact in his phone named Bianca. Through their conversation it was clear he was contemplating suicide.

There was a vivid, lengthy one where Malcolm was married to several men, all of which were extremely hairy, orangutan-like creatures. They lived together in a dwelling that was carved into the side of a limestone cliff wall. They seemed happy, eating their fire-roasted meat kabobs and playing music together on their primitive skin drums. When the sun began to set, she watched the ape navigate through a meadow of red reeds and climb atop a boulder overlooking their cave dwelling. In the distance, a vast city lit up the horizon, and thick smoke trails reached from the ground and up to the starry heavens. The ape sat for a while and watched the skinny, silver rockets launch periodically from the city, while munching on tart, orange berries it carried in a pouch made of skin that was a part of its large belly.

There was an exhilarating one where Malcolm was free-falling out of a helicopter and having problems with his parachute opening. The freezing air whipped his clothing loudly as he struggled to reach the emergency chute release. She could feel her heart pounding along with his as the adrenaline surged through his body. Luckily, it opened at the last second and he woke up shortly after landing.

There was another that was indiscernible, with waves of color and strange shapes cascading across her vision. She heard echoing tonal sounds all around her, and occasionally voices would converse in strange languages. The chaotic, swirling colors were beautiful but the constant motion made her feel nauseous. The notes on the dream hypothesized whoever they were watching was overdosing on hallucinogens.

Then there was an embarrassing one where he walked the halls of his college completely naked. She had heard of this being a commonly recurring dream for a lot of people. She even had a similar dream when she lived in Boston. While viewing the recording, she noticed that everyone else was naked as well, walking to class as though nothing was amiss.

Steph walked over to Malcolm's room to ask him about it. He explained that the naked dream was experienced so frequently by everyone that it must be a universe that formed extremely similarly to our own and was created at the exact same time. On that version of Earth, nudism is just a normal part of their culture.

Malcolm explained, "When we experience that dream it is embarrassing to us, but it is everyday life for them. Our brain is mostly just observing what is happening during the dream but will react on its own if what's happening is different enough from our perceived normative reality."

Steph said. "But how does the recording prove that the dream is actually happening in another universe?"

He took off his glasses and raised his eyebrows like he couldn't wait to tell her. "Samantha was the one that found it. The first Lexicon. It was in a lucid dream."

"She took control of the dream version of herself?"

"That's right, lucid dreamers command another version of themselves. Samantha was recording a dream about a year ago when she realized she was dreaming. This allowed her to consciously search for information about the world around her. Samantha walked over to her bookshelf and grabbed an encyclopedia off the shelf. She turned through every page, slow enough to be sure it would be clearly recorded. She got through the whole thing before waking up."

"An encyclopedia?"

"Containing an entire other world's worth of data. It was the clearest picture painted of another civilized world in all of history. The recording was transcribed into a file. It was in a new language, but we decoded it."

She felt him send her the file path in her mind and opened the Lexicon. She read every word of it as quickly as she could, learning thousands of new terms, animals, cultures, vehicles, geography, history; all of the definitions that were unique to that version of Earth.

"Since then, we've found more of them and cataloged all kinds of literature. In one case we captured hundreds of internet pages which were invaluable. Science books are the most fascinating to me as they show us the compositional variations of each universe and the exact differences in the elements."

Several more Lexicons were sent to her and she opened all of them, dedicating the separate processors in her brain to scan through each one. She watched as the multiverse blossomed in her mind, each branch growing its own unique piece of fruit - a larger structure, bound loosely by vast filaments stretching across space-time. She predicted and quantified the multiverse in her mind using each Lexicon, making a crude map of both the separate universes and the multitude of duplicates overlapping each other. She wondered how enormously complex the map could become as they discovered more Lexicons. Suddenly she smelled something burning. Smoke began to trail out of Steph's nostrils and was floating off the tip of her nose.

"Steph!" Malcolm called out and grabbed her shoulders. "Stop it, you're overheating."

Steph ceased her thoughts and tried to let the data and the meaning of the discovery fade from her active processes. She took deep breaths until there was no more smoke. "Sorry, I couldn't stop. That was the most fascinating thing I've ever seen. Holy shit. The other universes really are out there."

He let go of her and sighed. "I know. A brain could never create so much data so perfectly in such a short amount of time. The Lexicons are real, and we need more of them. If you ever have a lucid dream, try to remember to do some espionage. The paradigm of universes is an unending source of intelligence."

She browsed through the Lexicon database and stopped at one titled "Paradigm Extended Code." She opened it and slowly reviewed the code, being careful not to overheat her processors.

"What's this one?" she asked. "You found code for Paradigm in another universe?"

"That was another one Samantha found. She dreamt she was here, in this building, and asked a version of you to show her the code for Paradigm. We documented it and implemented it, saving us years of work.”

Steph gasped and said, “You stole the code from a future version of me?”

“Samantha did,” he laughed. “I considered that to be your actual first interview for the company. I had already seen what you were capable of. Now you can work on expanding the code that you’ve already designed.”

“I was wondering why the code was so…readable to me.” She stopped reviewing the code and locked eyes with him. “If Samantha and I work together in other universes, maybe we do too.” She smiled at him and asked, “Have you ever dreamt about me?”

His face turned red. He hesitated, then responded, “Yes, I’ve seen us all working together too.”

She smiled at him, but felt annoyed that he wasn’t giving her any details.

“That’s fine, if you don’t want to tell me, I’ll watch them myself,” she said and walked down the long corridor back to her room.

In the days that followed, Steph was caught in a whirlwind of clashing realities as she binge-watched hundreds more of Malcolm, Samantha, and her own dream recordings. Her formative perceptions of existence and meaning were shattered. She began to understand that everyone truly lives within a paradigm of existences, inextricably linked through the quantum realm. She also realized that when exploring an infinite multiverse, literally anything was possible. She kept watching, but never saw herself in any of Malcolm’s dream recordings.

During a particularly long viewing session, she saw Malcolm being hunted by a pack of vicious quadrupedal beasts, similar to giant wolves. She watched him lying on his back in the snow as they tore at him, pulling his body back and forth. He called out for help but it never came. Witnessing this gruesome death was particularly disturbing for her and she decided she needed some air. She left the Theater and went to the elevator, tapping the button that read 'Skywatch'. The elevator lurched and climbed all the way to the top of the mountain above the complex.

She stepped out onto the platform and breathed in the cool evening air. She was still getting used to how thin the air was, and only went outside when the sun wasn't blaring overhead. The cloudless skies here made it far too bright outside, far too often, compared to the dreary cloud cover she grew up with in Massachusetts. But the sun was setting behind the great peaks to the west, and the sky was painted in incredible hues of orange and purple. She walked across the wide platform over to the railing and took in the view.

"Now *that's* a sunset," a voice came from the adjacent side of the platform.

Steph turned toward the voice and saw that it was Samantha. "Yeah, it really is beautiful," she replied weakly. "But...it feels less special knowing there are so many sunsets out there that are exactly like it."

"Is something on your mind?" Samantha asked.

Steph wasn't sure if she was being genuine or just trying to get into her head to further her research, but she decided to give her the benefit of the doubt.

"Sorry for being a downer, Samantha. There is way too much on my mind."

"Call me Sam, please. It's what you call me in the other universes."

Steph looked perplexed and said, "I guess I can do that, Sam."

"It's so weird, actually standing next to you." Sam looked at Steph in awe. "I feel like you're already my friend."

"I wish I knew more about you," Steph said. "This is all too much sometimes. I feel like I can't process what all of it means."

"I know the feeling," Sam said. "Each universe we visit expands what we accept as reality by leaps and bounds. But with each one, we realize what we thought were the limits of possibility before has suddenly been proven wrong. It's hard to find the ground when it keeps moving."

Steph looked up at the faint stars and recognized Venus hiding between two peaks. "Glad to know *someone* gets it. Lately, I can't stop thinking about death. If one of our 'selves' dies, the link to the other self is broken and they don't even know. It doesn't even matter or affect them."

"Until now. I've been very affected by witnessing the death of my other selves," Sam said grimly.

"I wish there was something we could do to save them." Steph paused and decided to continue. "Before I came here, I thought my life was unique to me. But I don't even own *that*. My life is divided into the smallest of pieces; shared by so many others. It's not special in any way. It's not mine. I feel like I have no idea who I am."

"I know what you mean. But look at it this way, new universes are created every day. A new you was just born, seconds ago, somewhere out there, and billions of years from now it will still be happening. When you die, it's only this version of you that has died. Just a small part of the larger you that will live on seemingly forever in some form."

Samantha walked over and stood next to Steph, following her gaze to the emerging band of The Milky Way, dashed from horizon to horizon like countless scattered diamonds sparkling in the moonlight.

Samantha put her hand on Steph's shoulder to pull her gaze from the stars and said, "I've always felt small when looking up at the stars. Now that I know about the other universes, I actually feel larger. Like I'm actually part of something, like I matter. Your life is unique to this universe, Steph. You own that piece of yourself that no one can take from you. You can do anything you want to with it."

"I guess you're right. We aren't alone, we're a piece of a larger puzzle; a link in a chain." Steph smiled and turned back towards the sky. "Thanks, Sam" she said with the light from billions of stars bending across her teary eyes.

Over the next few months, Steph tackled the task of viewing the recordings using only the neural link. Through countless trial-and-error tests of the input streams translating into

Paradigm, encoding everything, and outputting it into another neural link for viewing, she was able to transcribe all five senses interpreted directly by the brain and the central processors. Dreams could now be viewed straight from her bedroom using her Buffer and no longer relied on the Theater.

There were still glitches to iron out, but Malcolm was impressed by her work and was sure they would finish ahead of schedule. Working with Sam, Steph also figured out how to interpret and relay all of the emotions the dreamer was experiencing, and transmit them through the appropriate parts of the brain. This made each viewing far more immersive, and, in some cases, far more frightening. Steph had to be more cautious about which dreams she was viewing as some of them were so impactful on her psyche she couldn't sleep for days.

One evening she sat at her desk and auto-connected to her Buffer. She was planning to do some diagnostics to make sure the glitches weren't caused by invalid data counts. She compared file counts to make sure there weren't any discrepancies in the recording process and noticed there were only 742 recordings logged under Malcolm's name. She remembered, with perfect clarity thanks to the AI implant, that Malcolm said he had recorded over 900 dreams. She decided if Malcolm had access to all of her dreams then it was only fair that she should see all of his, so she went looking for them.

She zipped through thousands of folders in her mind, searching every corner of the Paradigm storage system, but couldn't find the missing dreams. She decided another diagnostic to find discrepancies in file sizes might help. After running the numbers, she found a large swath of files that were unaccounted for in the storage counts. The files were encrypted and couldn't be accessed from outside the system. She would have to go into Paradigm to look for them.

She booted Paradigm and stood on the pillar platform that overlooked the virtual waterfalls again. She glanced around, but didn't see any interface to access the hidden files. There was nothing but vast oceans in all directions, and nothing she could see in the skies overhead. Then she looked over the edge of the pillar. About a hundred feet down she noticed a small opening that looked like a dilapidated doorway.

"There it is," she said softly. She lowered herself off the edge and gripped the vines that suffocated the pillar. She cautiously climbed down until she reached it, then swung her body into the opening. There was a file icon floating there, and she saw it was named "For Steph". She hesitated for a moment, then opened it up.

Inside were hundreds of dreams. She set the preferred point of view to third person and opened the first recording, titled "First Date". Her avatar stood next to a 1973 red Camaro parked in a clearing in the woods. Two people were laying on the hood and staring at the stars. She squinted in the darkness and saw they were Malcolm and another version of herself. Malcolm rolled onto his side and put his hand on her hip.

"I'm sorry for everything," he said to her. "I know that we will be happy together. Statistically speaking—" She interrupted him with a quick kiss.

"I know," she said.

He leaned in slowly and began to kiss her. She kissed him back, leaning into him and grazing her fingers on the back of his smooth head. Steph quickly closed the recording and sat cross-legged on the floor of the digital cave.

"He does dream about me," she said under her breath. The date stamp on the file icon was from three years ago. "But these were recorded...before I came here."

She loaded another recording and saw the two of them making breakfast together in a quaint single-story home filled with the natural light of the morning. Malcolm held up the spatula as he was talking with her and she noticed a wedding ring on his finger. She glanced over to the other version of herself, and she was wearing a diamond ring. In a different dream they were snowboarding down a mountain together in a resort in Colorado called Keystone. In another they were embracing passionately in front of a fireplace as snow fell outside the cabin window.

She hesitantly loaded one titled "Kids" and was transported to a green park on a sunny springtime day. She watched Malcolm and the 'other' Steph, who looked slightly older, as they playfully chased their children, a young boy and girl, around the grass.

Steph snapped from third-person into the vantage point of Malcolm, to view the rest of the recording from his perspective. The new perspective allowed her to feel exactly what he was feeling when it was originally recorded. He laid on the grass and their daughter laid across his chest, laughing and tapping her small fingers on his chin. Steph was blindsided by the overwhelming happiness he was feeling. She experienced such an intense feeling of love and knew it was far stronger than anything she had ever felt. She couldn't believe he was capable of feeling a love so pure and true.

As the recording ended, Steph cried at the sudden loss of that feeling. She rocked back and forth on the pixelated stone floor, hugging herself with her arms. She wanted to feel her daughter's warmth in her arms again, but there was nothing there but empty space. The intense feeling of loss panged within her chest and she couldn't get it to leave her.

She decided to try to move past her suffocating loneliness by watching more recordings. She loaded one more and watched her and Malcolm sitting at a bar as an emo punk band played from the stage. The couple was younger, in their early twenties by the look of his leather jacket and full head of black hair and her short, spiky rocker cut that was clearly colored blue with cheap, over-the-counter box dye. He ordered two whiskey sours, set one in front of her, and slurred, "I'll get my baby her favorite drink whenever she wants." They nuzzled together between the bar stools and started making out.

She pulled away and gazed into his eyes. "I can't wait to be done with this place. We'll graduate in May, and finally be done with NYU. We can finally start our research."

"I can't believe Sam got the research grant. Today we start the triumvirate!" he called out and raised his glass high above his head.

"Sam!" Steph called out towards the crowd. A girl in a black dress and long brown hair turned around and waved to her, then blew a kiss. Steph yelled to her, "Triumvirate!" and blew a kiss back. She wrapped her arms around Malcolm's neck again.

He gave her a kiss and said, "I don't need to record my dreams, I'm living them." A carefree smile grew across his face and he continued, "But I'm so down to go to Colorado."

She kissed him back and said, "This whole thing was your idea. I just want to develop the VR platform. I thought of a name for it, want to know what it is?"

"Sure," he said and drank his whiskey. "Whatcha got?"

"Let's call it...Paradigm."

He nodded slowly and said, "Paradigm. Love it, babe. We're gonna change the world," They both smiled and kissed.

She ended the recording and quickly closed completely out of the recording.

She sat up in her Buffer and shakily stood to her feet. She couldn't stop the tears from streaming down her face. So many emotions flowed through her from the sheer beauty of what she had seen—and felt—but a rage of betrayal welled up inside her too, pushing the other emotions aside. Electricity popped in her head and she fell to her knees. The door to her room opened and Malcolm walked in, holding his hands behind his back with a serious look on his face. Steph rose to her feet immediately.

"What is this? I found your little stash of me," she shouted.

"I know," he said as he stopped walking.

She could smell the smoke in her nose. "So, what, these are just little virtual fantasies you created of me so you could get off?"

"They're far more than that. They are real dream recordings," Malcolm said. "Check the dates. I couldn't just tell you we were destined to be together without scaring you off. The only option was to show you everything I've discovered. To prove to you how compatible we are—how strong and rare our love is."

"You are a creep. Leave me the hell alone." Smoke trailed out of her ears in thin tendrils.

He winced. "Steph, I've been dreaming about you for years. I saw what we were capable of in so many other universes. I knew we could create Paradigm together. But more than that, I fell in love with you. I had to be with you in this universe too." He walked over to her and took her hands in his.

She shook her head, "Maybe you are telling the truth, but I don't know if I want to follow in the footsteps of my other selves. How can I be sure that path is the best for me?"

"None of us can ever know for sure," he said as his eyebrows sank. "But in our case, we can see that it works out for other versions of us. That's more than most people get. It isn't just a blind jump, we've seen that it can work. It's the closest thing possible to having a soulmate."

"I've never believed in destiny," she said, "and I didn't want to know all of that, about what the future could be like."

"I'm sorry, but I had to seek you out. We've already missed out on so much time together. I need you in my life. In *this* life, not in a recording."

"If they really are dreams, then these are other people, whole universes away. Not *us*, not in this universe. I'm not just a carbon copy of them, I'm my own person!" she yelled and stormed past him.

"I know you are," he said, watching as she stormed across the room. "You aren't that girl that hung out in dive bars with me, that studied at NYU with Sam and I. This universe is different. Sam and I met there in this one, but you were gone. I wish you were there."

Steph stopped as she grabbed the door knob.

He cleared his throat and said, "I've been searching for you since the first time I saw you. I recorded it, it's called 'Washington Square Park'. Did you watch it?"

"I'm done watching that shit. It fucks with my head," she said, walked out and slammed the door shut.

She took the elevator up and entered the garage at the surface. She walked between the rows of cars and got in the fastest, loudest car they had. She revved the Camaro's V8 and dropped the clutch, tearing out of the garage and onto the winding roads as the sun lingered above the mountains.

Her hair whipped out of the red convertible top like flames, painted in bright orange light from the setting sun. Her mind raged with thousands of thoughts, queries, and calculations, simultaneously compiling throughout her brain. No matter how much she beared down and forced the electricity into the over-clocked processors, she couldn't find the answers. After a few minutes, the cool mountain air rushing past her head had cooled her down a little.

She slowed down and tried to focus on one thing at a time. She knew she was asking herself the wrong questions. She simplified everything to the most basic question she could: Did she believe him? She pictured his face in her mind and tried to understand if he was telling the truth. She searched through all of her memories, back through the years before she came to Singularity.

Suddenly, a realization swept over her. In this universe, and nine hundred and sixty-four others, she pulled to the side of the road and stopped the car. She quickly reclined her seat, closed her eyes, and focused all of her processing power to boot up

Paradigm. The user interface flickered across her vision, then came into focus. She keyed "Washington Square Park" into the display.

The world swirled around her as the simulation built. A massive gray surface revealed itself, then sprouted grass that looked like a field of steel wool before it turned bright green and wet from the misting rain. On the horizon, buildings sprung from the ground and flashed with color in a mosaic of browns and grays. It was a park, surrounded by buildings, with a dull, clouded sky hanging overhead.

She let it play from Malcolm's perspective as he walked across the pavement. He threw the collar of his jacket up to keep the rain off his neck. He pulled the phone out of his pockets and checked the time. He started walking faster, rounding the pathway around Washington Square Arch. He looked up at the enormous arch, dropping his jaw in wonder, when he collided with her. The young woman's books scattered along the wet pavement. Malcolm bent down to help her, and she turned to look at him.

Steph was staring back at what looked like a ten-year younger version of herself. She had long hair with bangs, and her look of annoyance quickly disappeared when she saw him.

"Oh, I'm so sorry. I was looking up, completely spaced out. Let me help you," he said.

Steph changed to a third-person perspective to get a look at Malcolm.

He had a head full of long, straight hair that covered his forehead down to his eyes. He didn't wear glasses, and Steph immediately recognized his stone gray eyes. Seeing this young version of him, she remembered why he seemed familiar to her when she first saw him. She had seen him before they ever met, periodically throughout her entire life, in her dreams.

"Oh," the young Steph said and smiled nervously. "That's okay, I was doing the same thing. It's so beautiful here."

"I know what you mean," Malcolm said as he helped her up. "So beautiful."

Steph asked, "Are you new here too?"

"Yeah, just moved out here. This whole college thing is a bit intense."

"I know. It's like, how can a city that's so big feel so lonely?"

"I can keep you company," Malcom said. "Let me buy you a cup of coffee. I owe you that much."

"I don't want to go to class with wet books, so fine. Let's go on an adventure," she said and turned to walk with him. She grabbed his hand and slid her fingers between his, interlocking them.

Steph opened her eyes and sat up in her car seat. The chilly mountain wind gently moved her hair as she was overcome with a realization. At that moment, Malcolm felt more real to her than anyone in her entire life. She could feel his presence throughout her memories, and realized there was another force connecting the two of them, just as she was connected to the other versions of herself. Something had entangled her with Malcolm in each universe - their love for each other. They were like two stars in a binary system, each powerful and unrelenting, encircling each other in a cosmic dance forever. She felt a magnetization towards him, in every molecule of her being, and knew in her heart they were destined to be together.

She laughed excitedly and quickly called Malcolm.

"Steph?" he answered.

The sound of his voice in her mind comforted her. "Hey. I'm sorry I left, I just had to think things through. I'm coming back to pick you up, okay?"

He sighed with relief and said, "It's a date."

It Came from the Ceiling

It Came from the Ceiling

The tall Wasatch Maple trees along both sides of North Sherwood Street were afflicted by autumn but still clung to most of their broad, golden leaves. The evening sunshine cascaded from the western foothills across the town, split by the gaps in the granite formation known as Horsetooth Rock. In the gray lines between the brilliant orange foliage, a sky blue 1962 Ford Fairlane glided through the neighborhood. The father drove the car, the mother sat next to him, and the small boy shared the wide backseat with stacks of cardboard boxes. Question Mark and the Mysterians played "96 Tears" on the radio while the couple beamed excited smiles at each other.

"There it is!" The wife exclaimed while pointing to a modest bungalow on the right side of the street. "Our cozy little Colorado home."

The boy was enthralled by the sunlight brightening his mother's pale arms and crimson flower-patterned dress. He couldn't tear his gaze from her curls of auburn hair bouncing along her shoulders. The car rolled through the opening in the white picket fence into the cracked driveway. The husband killed the engine.

"We're finally here," he said, then stepped out of the car and rubbed his eyes.

He was a lanky man too tall for his pleated brown pants. His greasy brown hair was neatly combed and he wore thick black rectangular glasses. His eyes intently scanned the house for flaws.

The boy walked around the front yard, sheepishly looking at his new home. It was an old yellow house with white trim and a small dirt yard filled with weeds. It had half-buried, cracked stones leading from the driveway to the porch steps. The browned leaves of dying iris flowers sagged along the sidewalk and stirred in the wind. He missed their old house even though the air smelled cleaner here.

The wife sat on the swinging bench that hung from thin chains bolted to the roof of the porch. Her listless gaze wandered around the yard. The low light of the setting sun shone on her face, and lit the bruise on the side of her face. She sensed this and instinctively moved her hair forward to cover it. The boy noticed her melancholy and walked to the edge of the porch. She patted the cushion next to her and her son climbed up to join her.

The husband fiddled with the lock for a few minutes and swore under his breath. At last, the red door swung open and the family walked into the empty living room. The faded wooden floorboards creaked beneath their weight as they crossed toward the kitchen. The husband flipped the light switch and nothing happened.

"Must be burned out," he muttered.

"The floors are a bit creaky, dear," the wife said. She floated into the kitchen and ran her hand across the pea-green vinyl countertop.

"Sure, they creak a bit. They're the originals from 1915. At least the kitchen was redone recently."

"Oh, I know, don't you just love it?" she said while bringing her hands to her chest. "Let's bring the floors up to date as well. They're fifty years old after all. They look as if they're about to collapse."

He walked over to his wife, threw his arms around her waist, lifted her and spun in a slow circle. "One step at a time my dear." He smiled and kissed her rosy cheek. He set her down and said, "I'm going to start with fixing the light."

"Why don't you start with the bed frame so we have a place to sleep tonight?" she said, pushing him away.

"Is that all we're gonna do?" he said with a wink.

"Behave, darling," she said with a playful scowl. She turned to her son with an earnest smile and said, "What do you think, Charles? Do you like the house?"

The boy nodded. Approving his answer, the mother turned to the kitchen. The husband brought in a load of boxes from the car. The mother started cleaning and young Charles found the backdoor.

He walked into the cool air of the backyard past a pile of old blackened firewood stacked taller than he was. Chain link fences ran along the length of the yard, but the back edge of the yard was open. Through the open section, the dirt and weeds blended into a forest full of maples, aspen, juniper, and spruce. It smelled of pine needles with a hint of decay. He walked to the edge and gazed deep into the trees, wondering how far the twisted abyss sprawled before him.

Something caught his eye and he glanced downwards. Crawling across the white toe of his shoe was an earwig. He bent down and pinched its smooth body between his fingers. Its long spiky pincers on the end of its abdomen reminded him of alien monsters from the science fiction books he liked to read.

The boy watched and grinned as it struggled helplessly to escape his hold. It arched its abdomen back and forth until it clasped onto his finger with its pincers. He yelped and dropped it to the ground. He frantically inspected his finger but no skin was broken. As the insect crawled away, he raised his foot and stomped it into the dirt as hard as he could.

He slowly lifted his leg and saw the flattened insect was now motionless in death. He returned his gaze to the depths of the forest. The sun had set further and the trees were turning bluer and darker by the second. He heard the low, haunting hoot of an owl and scanned the treetops for it.

He saw something just behind a cluster of branches in one of the trees. It was a shape that he couldn't quite make out, but it was the same dark brown color of the tree bark and was perched maybe thirty feet up the tree. As he stared, it slowly backed away from him and floated through the trees. Three red lights along its belly rotated in a circle as it soared. All he heard was a few branches snap as it swiftly disappeared into the night sky.

The mystery of the bizarre sighting filled him with an intense panic. He turned on his heels and ran back toward the house as quickly as his skinny legs would take him. As he stopped to open the door, he turned to look back at the forest. There was no trace of the object, but he saw movement next to him and looked at the firewood piled at the back door. He stepped closer to the pile and saw hundreds of small, dark bodies crawling across the logs.

"Hey," a small voice called from behind him.

He turned to see a small red-haired boy with his hands clinging to the chain link fence.

"Whatcha running from?" The red-haired boy asked.

"Saw somethin' in the woods," Charles said. "It was floating around in the trees like a kite."

"Wudn't no kite," the boy said. "I seen it before. I think it's an angel."

"Looked more like a devil to me," Charles said.

"Well, I seen it flying around the roof of your house before. It scared the neighbors so bad they up and moved." The boy wriggled his nose and sniffed.

"Keep an eye out for it, wouldya?" Charles asked.

The boy nodded.

"I have to go inside now. See you around," Charles said.

He walked through the door and unintentionally slammed it shut behind him. The house was warm and comforting to him. His mother was preparing dinner and his father had just finished constructing the bed frame for their mattress. Then he saw his father storming across the room towards him.

"Charles," his father's voice was loud and angry. "What the hell do you think you're doing?" He strode over to his son and grabbed his shirt collar. "Don't slam the door shut or you'll break the frame." He leaned his head down so close to Charles' face that he could smell the alcohol on his breath. "Do you understand me, boy? Don't just stare at me, use your words like a man, you little–"

There was a knock at the front door. The father let go of his son and went to answer it. Charles followed his father to the door while angrily wiping the tears from his red face. His father opened the door and its hinges cried out in pain.

A man stood in the yellow porchlight to greet them. He wore a black suit and tie with a white undershirt; a black derby with round-frame eyeglasses, and his face was clean-shaven. He looked to be in his fifties with laugh lines creased beneath his kind eyes. Miller moths, drunk from the light, flew in clumsy loops around him.

"How do you do? My name is Detective Frank Goslin," he said in a deep, authoritative voice and extended his hand.

The husband shook it and said, "How do ya do?"

"A real life detective?" Charles asked.

"Don't worry, I don't have a warrant," he said with a re-assuring smile. "I just wanted to stop by and welcome you to the neighborhood. I live four houses down that-a-way. It's the gray house, number one twenty-eight. "

"It's nice to meet you. We're the Chandlers, my wife Jill there, and my son Charles here. I'm Kenneth. We just moved across the country from Connecticut."

"Oh, you'll love it here in Fort Collins. If you can tolerate the dumb shit college students crying about the war, anyway."

Kenneth laughed and tried to change the subject, "Are you married?"

"I was, until recently. Cancer took my wife," he said solemnly.

"I'm sorry to hear that," Kenneth said.

"It would get us all eventually, if given the time," he said. He shifted his weight back on his heels and forward again.

"I suppose so," Kenneth said with a crease between his brows. "Any kids?" He asked, immediately regretting it.

"I'm afraid not," he replied and swallowed.

"Well, somedays I sure wish I didn't," Kenneth said while rustling Charles' hair. The boy pouted and walked away while smoothing his hair back into place.

"Anyway, I just wanted to introduce myself. If you ever need anything don't hesitate to stop on by," he said and waved a hand at Jill standing in the kitchen. She waved back and Kenneth closed the door.

Later that evening, Kenneth started a fire in the living room fireplace. The family sat on the floor together on a blanket Jill had spread across the floor and watched the flames quietly lap at the air. Charles had fallen asleep laying in his mother's lap, and the couple looked into each other's eyes. Then a loud thump was heard over their heads.

"What was that?" Jill asked.

"Probably a broken branch landing on the roof. Don't worry about it, darling."

Kenneth reached his hand out and grazed her cheek, then grabbed the back of her head and kissed her. Jill opened her eyes briefly enough to see something black was crawling down the sleeve of his arm towards her face. She recoiled and rose to her feet while holding Charles on her hip.

"There's something on your arm," she cried out and pointed. Kenneth glanced at his arm and quickly slapped the insect off of it. He leaned over and saw it skittering cattywampus across the floor.

"It's just an earwig. They don't bite," he said while pressing the toe of his loafer down and feeling the crunch of its carapace buckling.

"I don't care if they bite or not. They're dreadful," Jill said. She looked down at Charles and asked him if he was okay.

"Yes momma. I saw some of those things outside," he said drearily and turned to look at his father. Jill noticed there was one on the top of Charles' head, aimlessly crawling across his auburn hair. She screamed and brushed it off quickly using the sleeve of her dress.

"Kenneth! There was one on him," she whined. "One on our boy!"

Kenneth's eyes darted around the floor. He saw another one sitting still near the wall. A few more hid between cracks in the floorboards. Yet another crawled up the wall in the corner. He saw a group of them enter through the gap under the front door. He looked up to watch four of them crawling along the ceiling. They hung from their hind legs and writhed their front sections around as if detecting the scent of the bodies below them. They released themselves and dropped from the ceiling; their hard bodies striking the floor like the soft pattering of rain. Kenneth started stomping the pests with his boots with frantic panic.

Jill noticed one near her feet. She stepped backward to get away from it, then felt something tickling her knee. She saw it briefly before it disappeared under the seam of her dress. It climbed higher up her leg and grasped her inner thigh with its six scratchy legs. She reached into her dress and grabbed it in the palm of her hand, then screamed and flung it towards the wall.

She clutched Charles tightly and ran into his bedroom, then leapt onto his bed. From her vantage point, she analyzed the room and tried to catch her breath. There weren't any of them around that she could see, so she laid in bed with Charles and gently ran her fingers through his hair, expecting to find one with each stroke. The boy breathed steadily, trying to calm himself down. He remembered the earwig in the forest and regretted killing it. He buried his face in the pillow, too ashamed to tell his mother what he had done.

Jill could hear her husband stomping around every now and then, and occasionally saw one or two of the devilish pests creeping across the carpet under the bed. She hated the way they walked; so clearly lacking intelligence and purpose. She was convinced they existed simply to annoy her. She was sure she felt one on her neck, but couldn't find anything with her frantic grabs. She kept shaking her long hair to make sure none were hiding in the curls. After convincing herself there weren't any of them crawling on her, she eventually drifted into slumber.

The next morning, Kenneth opened the bedroom door to find his family sleeping. Jill woke from the door opening and sat up in bed.

"I killed a lot of those bastards. Swept them up and threw them out. You can come out now," he said drearily.

"Thank you dear," she said and rubbed her green eyes. She walked over to him and scratched the underside of his chin. "Let Charles sleep. I'll make us some breakfast."

"Good, I'm starved. I'm gonna work on fixing that light," he replied and walked into the living room. He grabbed a step ladder and placed it below the light fixture on the ceiling. He unscrewed the lightbulb and started to screw in the new one, wincing at the sound of metal scraping metal.

He suddenly felt something on his arm and instinctively brushed it, but nothing was there. He thought he felt one crawling on his leg, but lifted his pant leg and there was nothing there either. He shook off the paranoia and returned to his work. He screwed the lightbulb in completely, walked down the ladder, and flipped the light switch. Nothing happened.

"I'm gonna have to take this whole damn thing apart," he muttered to himself and went back up the ladder.

In the kitchen, Jill pulled a frying pan out of the cupboard. Underneath it were several earwigs that had curled up in the comfort of darkness. With their shelter gone, they stirred and began to slowly scatter. Jill slammed the pan down again on top of them.

"Darling! There are more in the cupboards," she called out to him. She walked over to the sink and rinsed the back of the pan off. She watched their mangled black bodies swirl in circles before succumbing to the drain. "I think we'd better call an exterminator, don't you?"

Kenneth ignored her and focused on removing the light fixture. He finally removed all of the screws and pulled the light fixture out of the ceiling. He could see the inside of the attic through the hole in the ceiling and inspected the wiring leading into the light. He saw there were damaged wires that looked like they had been chewed on by something.

He walked down the stepladder and turned towards his messy toolbox. After some fruitless rummaging for a wire cutter, he produced a flask from his shirt pocket. Behind him something emerged from the hole in the ceiling. It was the tail end of an enormous earwig, much larger than the others, clasping its sharp pincers open and closed as it moved. Kenneth took a hearty swig of whiskey from the flask, unaware of its presence. It sagged its long abdomen two feet out of the opening, grasping blindly through the air with its pincers until they found the side of Kenneth's neck.

The sharp prongs pierced his flesh easily and gripped it strongly. He cried out, dropping his flask to the floor, but the insect latched onto him. Its abdomen convulsed frantically. He could feel a thick substance pump into his bloodstream as he flew into a full panic. He leapt from the ladder, bringing the entire insect out of the hole and they crashed to the floor. It writhed and wrapped itself around Kenneth's head. He grabbed it with all of his might and managed to pry it off. He pulled it away from him at arm's length and felt the pincers slide out from his neck. He scrambled to his feet and flung the massive insect to the ground.

Jill was standing by his side holding the frying pan with ghost-white terror on her face. He held his bloody neck with one hand and grabbed the frying pan from her with the other. He bounded forward and bashed the insect with the pan against the floor. At the moment his swing made impact, hundreds of smaller white insects exploded off of its back and skittered in all directions.

"Christ," he yelled and stumbled backwards. "It was carrying babies!"

Jill screamed and ran away. Kenneth became enraged and swung the pan over and over against the ground until all of the little white insects were nothing but smears in the dents in the wood. He slumped to his knees and breathed heavily as he looked down at the slaughter.

The creature looked like a stone-gray earwig with dark brown stripes along its three-foot length. However, it was plumper than an earwig, with huge fangs extending from its mouth, and smelled like stagnant pond water. Bright yellow juice oozed from the tears along its body which slowly seeped into the hardwood floor.

"Jill?" he said gruffly. "Call the exterminator."

Later that evening, Kenneth laid in the master bedroom with a wet cloth draped on his forehead. Jill had stopped the bleeding and bandaged the two pencil-sized holes in his neck. She sat on the bedside next to him and changed out the cloth for a fresh one. He was sweating, but he assured her that he felt okay. She heard the exterminator knocking on the door and went to let him in.

He was a hefty man and wore a uniform consisting of a gray shirt, green trousers, and matching cap that read "Jim's Pest

Removal." His shirt had faint sweat stains in both armpits, and he wore leather gloves. The name tag stitched above his shirt pocket read "Jim".

"Hello sir, we have quite the pest problem. My husband was attacked."

"Attacked? You said it was an earwig."

"Yes, some kind of giant mutant earwig. Come in! Let me show you."

She walked him into the living room and pointed at the felled beast. "It came from the ceiling."

He approached it cautiously with his thumbs tucked into his tool belt. Crouching down to get a better look, the exterminator rubbed his chin with confusion "What in the hell?"

He took a pencil from his shirt pocket, slid it under one side of the insect, and lifted it slowly until it flipped onto its back.

"It...looks kinda like an earwig. Got dem prongs on its ass anyways, pardon my French. But earwigs don't have fangs like this, and could never get this big. I ain't never seen nothin' like this, ma'am."

"It bit my husband," she said, biting the nail of her pointer finger.

"Well, if it has fangs here that means it's venomous. You should get a doctor over here to check on him. I don't have any antivenom on me, I regret to inform."

"It wasn't the fangs – he said it stabbed him with the horns on the other end."

"Oh, well maybe it was trying to lay eggs or somethin'. Unless these are stingers kinda like a wasp's, but I ain't never seen an insect with two stingers," he said and pulled his thick mustache into his mouth with his bottom lip.

"Well, I know it was already carrying babies. See them scattered across the floor? Would it already be laying more eggs?'

"I see 'em. Not likely this soon, but y'know, I don't know anything about this thing. Best if I take it over to the bio lab at CSU and see if they can identify it. Maybe someone brought the sucker up from Brazil or somethin'. It definitely shouldn't be here."

"It's all yours," Jill said. The exterminator slid the creature into a small burlap sack.

"Alrighty, I'll get outta your hair now," he said, standing to his feet. "I'll tell someone at the lab to contact you when they know somethin'."

The man left and Jill returned to the bedroom to check on her husband. The bedroom was pitch black, but she could see his chest raising and falling slowly.

"Did you show him the body?" he asked.

"Yes, dear. He is taking it to the lab to get it identified. He had no idea what it was," she sat on the bed next to him.

"Fuckin' thing." He started coughing and rolled onto his side. She sat next to him.

"Let me take a look at the wound, dear. He said it may have even laid eggs. Horrid creatures, reproducing like that."

Jill leaned in closer to him and slowly peeled the bandage away from the wound. It looked like two pock marks that were swollen shut. She didn't find any protrusions or visible eggs. She pressed the bandage back into place.

"It looks okay. He said I should call a doctor for you, but I know how to make you feel better," she said while running her fingers softly across his stomach. She got up and closed the door, then turned him onto his back and climbed on top of him.

Afterwards, she got up and turned on the lamp on the bedside table. In the yellow light, she saw that there was a streak of blood on the pillow. She leaned down to inspect it and noticed there were three white molars at the base of the pillow.

"Kenneth," she exclaimed, "I think you've lost some of your teeth!"

He sat up at the noise and turned to face her. He had blood smeared around his mouth and lazily tried to rub it off with his hand. He looked dazed as if he was struggling to process what was happening.

"Kenneth?" she asked.

His gaze fell to the teeth lying on the bed as he slowly realized they were his own. He opened his mouth slowly and put his hand into his mouth to check his teeth. Thin, sharp, black fangs poked through his gums, filling the holes where his teeth had been. He pressed on each fang with his fingers and they punctured his fingertips easily. Jill's eyes bulged and her mouth hung open, terrified of what she was watching. He kept poking new holes as blood ran down his hands.

"Stop it! You're cutting yourself," she said while pulling down on his arms.

"What... Jill? What is happening to me?" he asked with pain in each word, barely able to pronounce them.

"Just stay here and lie back down! I'll call the doctor right away." She scooped the teeth off of the bed and put them in her dress pocket, then replaced the bloody pillow with a fresh one. She walked into the kitchen and called the doctor on the pale-yellow rotary phone fastened to the wall. Her hands were shaking so badly she had to redial it four times.

She opened the red front door for the doctor who was caught yawning. He wore a gray overcoat with a matching derby and carried a brown leather medical briefcase. The moon watched menacingly from the foothills, casting its blue light across the frigid branches above the house. With a tip of his hat, the doctor stepped out of the cold night air and into the warm, welcoming home.

"Hello ma'am, I'm Doctor Martin. I believe you spoke to my assistant on the telephone?"

"Yes, sir. Thank you for coming out so late. I didn't think it could wait until morning. My husband is... not well."

"Yes, my assistant provided a most outlandish report. You said your husband is losing teeth? Has he been brushing them?" he said, shooting her a crooked smile.

"No, it isn't like that. I know it sounds crazy, but there are sharp black things in his mouth that are...growing in. He lost these three teeth," she said as she fished them from her pocket and held them out in the flat of her palm.

He creased his brow and peered at them. "I see. They don't seem decayed. Quite unusual to lose a healthy tooth, aside from physical trauma knocking them out, of course. Did you two get into a fight?"

"No, nothing like that," she said and placed the teeth back into her dress pocket.

"Good. Can you take me to him?"

"Yes, he's in the bedroom, I'll show you."

He reached out and held her from the shoulder. "Would you look at this, you've got a child on the way, haven't you? How wonderful," he said with a broad smile.

With his other hand, he gently touched his pointer finger to her stomach. She looked down at it and held it with her hands. It had grown into a small but noticeable bump.

"Oh... yes. It must've just...I mean, yes, we're very happy," she said.

"Congratulations my dear. Looks to be a few months along. Have you been to the doctor yet?" he asked.

"No, not yet."

"Well, you can schedule checkups through my assistant if you need to. Always better to be safe after all."

She nodded and turned away. They walked through the living room, past Charles' room where he was sound asleep, and over to the master bedroom door. She opened the door and walked over to the bedside lamp. The room was filled with light when she pulled the pearl chain lamp switch. Kenneth was lying on his side facing away from the light.

"Hello, my name is Doctor Martin. Come on lad, let's have a look at you," he said and placed his hand on Kenneth's shoulder. Kenneth turned toward him and sat up. He was sweating and his skin was bland and grayish. His mouth hung slack-jawed and his eyes were bloodshot.

"Your wife tells me you aren't feeling so hot. Can you tell me what happened?"

"I was bitten," Kenneth said and weakly tapped on his bandaged neck. "By something...was it a snake?"

"Dear," Jill chimed over the Doctor's shoulder. "Don't you remember? It was a bug. An earwig type thing. They've taken it away for testing."

The doctor contorted his face and clarified, "An earwig?'

"An... earwig... was it?" Kenneth muttered.

"I seriously doubt it." the doctor said while popping the clasp on his leather bag open. "I can redress your neck wound. But first, let's take a look at these teeth of yours. Open up, say aaah."

Kenneth's head fell backwards and rested against his back. His jaw shifted open, extending all the way down to his collar bones, revealing hundreds of small, sharp fangs poking out of his gums and the roof of his mouth. His human teeth, which had been floating in the crevices of his mouth, spilled out and down his shirt. The teeth rolled and bounced across the carpet as Kenneth sat silently with bloody drool dripping in strings from his gaping head.

The doctor sprung to his feet and stepped backwards, fixated on the rows of strange new teeth. He shook his head in absolute disbelief. Jill covered her mouth and stepped out into the hallway.

"Good heavens! You...you...your DNA has somehow...mutated," The doctor stammered. "You are...he is a new species. This is impossible. I'll have to take a blood sample and get it over to the lab post haste." The doctor produced a syringe from his bag with shaking hands.

Kenneth didn't react. The doctor pulled Kenneth's soggy shirt sleeve up, but gripped too hard and a layer of grayish skin slid up his arm with it. Kenneth moaned in pain and started making quiet gurgling sounds. A few centimeters beneath the slogged off skin was a shiny black layer of new skin.

"My boy," the doctor said with a bewildered look. "You seem to be...molting your skin off. I've never seen anything--" he trailed off.

He pressed the needle firmly against the fresh, tender, scaly flesh, gave it more pressure, and it finally poked through with a slight popping noise. Kenneth suddenly lurched forward and slammed his numerous fangs into the doctor's neck, biting deep into his flesh as the warm metallic blood rushed in his mouth. The doctor cried out; his scream abruptly silenced as Kenneth continued to chew through his throat in aggressive, animalistic bites. Jill screamed and slammed the door shut.

She sat on the dirty white linoleum floor with her back against the kitchen counter and cried. She could still hear the struggling, but knew there was no way to stop her husband from murdering the doctor. He was beyond saving after that first attack. She suddenly noticed blood was pooling under the door.

She stood and ran to the phone, picked up the handset and frantically rotated the dial. It rang a few times before a woman answered on the other side.

"Hello?"

"Mom, it's Jill," she said between breaths.

"Oh hello, darling. How is the new place?"

"Mom, can you come get me right now? I need to leave."

"You just moved four hundred miles away from your loving mother, breaking her heart, and now you want me to drive all that way to come get you? Have you lost your mind?"

"I'm sorry, mother. Kenneth is horribly sick and I need to leave. And...I'm pregnant."

There was a pause of dead air, then her mother replied, "You have a son with Kenneth, he is sick, you are pregnant with his child, and you want to leave him? Dear, a wife's duty is to his husband. I won't have a daughter that's a divorcee, you hear me? It's an abomination to God. Now take care of your husband while he is ill. Don't be an embarrassment. Goodbye."

A click signaled she had hung up on her. She weakly set the handset into its receptacle. Around the corner came Charles. He saw his mother there and walked to comfort her. She ran towards him and scooped him up in her arms. She ran with him to the living room and sat on the floor against the wall next to the red front door.

"Are you okay, Mommy? You look sad," Charles asked with fright in his voice as he wiped a tear from her red cheek.

"Daddy is really sick," she said.

"Is he going to get better?"

She nodded her head. "He's not going to go away. He'll get better...we...just have to give him some time to heal. I won't let anyone take him away. I won't let you grow up without a father," she said between nervous breaths.

Charles started crying and she held his head against her breast. "Don't worry. He'll get better. But promise me something, okay?" She lifted his head and made him look her in the eyes. He wiped his tears away as she said, "Don't go in the bedroom. It's off limits. If you go in there, you'll get sick too."

"I won't go in there, Mommy," he said and sobbed.

"Promise me," she shouted and shook him by the shoulders.

"I promise," he said while nodding.

As they sat there caressing, earwigs scuttled across the floor around them. She could feel them crawling across her shirt but was too overwhelmed to care. She stood and carried Charles back to his bedroom and laid with him. She could feel the insects crawling in her curls but decided to leave them.

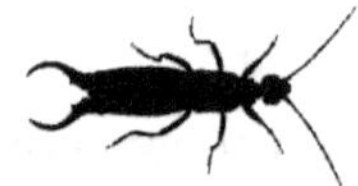

A few days passed and one morning Jill awoke to the kitchen telephone. She shuffled into the kitchen with her big stomach sticking out of her bathrobe and answered it. She held the phone up to her disheveled, unwashed hair.

"Hello?"

"Hello Mrs. Chandler, how are you? This is Detective Goslin, we met the other day?"

"Yes, I believe you spoke with my husband."

"Yes ma'am. I'm calling about a missing person case: Doctor Martin. His assistant said he went over to your house on a call. Wife says he never made it home and reported him missing a few days ago."

"Missing?" Jill said empathetically. "How terrible. I'm afraid I haven't seen him. He left our house after checking on my husband, that's the last I've spoken to him."

"Thank you, ma'am. His assistant said your husband was sick, that he'd been bitten by something. Sounds something awful, how is he?"

"Oh, yes. A spider bit him while he was up working on the light fixture."

"Oh? He also said that your husband had lost some teeth, is that right?"

"Yes, well you see," she hesitated. "When he was bitten, he fell and... knocked a few of his teeth out on the stepladder. It was an awful accident. The doctor checked on him and now he's doing great. He's off and back at work now. Everything is perfectly fine."

"Well, that's good to hear. Have a good afternoon now and give me a ring if you remember anything that might help me find the good doctor, okay? Bye bye now."

Jill hung up the phone and walked over to the bedroom door quietly. She pressed her ear to the door but didn't hear any sounds.

"Kenneth?" she said quietly. "Are you feeling any better?"

There was only silence beyond the door.

"Please, honey, please get better. Don't leave me all alone," she said as she ran her fingers gently across the smooth white paint on the door.

"Meat," Kenneth said through the door, making her jump. "Meat," he repeated in a deeper, gravelly voice.

"Okay darling," she replied. "I'll run to the market and get you some food. Just stay put."

Jill and Charles took the Fairlane over to the local grocer a few blocks away called Beaver's Market. Her hands were shaking slightly, but she kept her composure, smiling and nodding at the other shoppers as she rushed to the butcher's counter. She picked up three beef round roasts; the biggest ones they had. Charles picked out some candy corn and Sugar Cones cereal. They checked out at the line with an older woman running the register. She was wearing a black and orange witch outfit, and eyed Jill up and down while taking drags of her cigarette.

"Getting some candy for Halloween, boy?" she asked hoarsely.

Charles nodded at the woman.

She smiled at Jill with yellow teeth and said to her, "I see another one is on the way. Good for you. By the looks of you, maybe got a month or two left?" Jill tried to smile, but could not, and she couldn't respond. The older woman shrugged and they finished the transaction in silence.

She took the groceries home and told Charles to go to his bedroom for a nap. He shuffled to his bedroom. She put the milk away and unwrapped the roasts, then slowly approached the closed bedroom door.

"Darling, can I come in? I'm so worried about you," she said meekly.

She creaked open the door; sliding into view were human bones scattered across the floor. The carpet was black with blood and the room smelled musty and rotten. The mattress was torn apart with a wide hole dug into the middle of it. Kenneth was curled up within the hole.

He rose from it like a devil emerging from hell. Black exo-skeleton plates had formed all along his back and sides; his torso had grown several feet longer. His arms grew black in color and now were covered in short, hard spikes. He crawled to the floor, slithering out of his den until his elongated body fully emerged. He towered over her by three feet and stared at her with glossy, yellowed eyes. His face, now wet with tears, had changed more similarly to the sharp, angular face of an insect. Long mandibles grew from his cheeks on each side of his head. Black, sectioned antennae had sprouted from the top of his now-hairless head. They twitched and whipped through the air in search of her.

"Oh Kenneth," she said with a whimper. She glanced down at the floor, unable to look at him directly. "I got some roasts for you. How do you... do you want them prepared?"

"Meat," Kenneth said hoarsely and sharply, like a wolf's snarl. "Meat. Now." Saliva dripped from his gaping black mouth; the long strings dangled in front of her face.

Jill stepped out into the kitchen and picked up all three roasts in her arms. She walked back into the bedroom and Kenneth snatched one out of her arms. She dropped the others to the floor and stepped away fearfully. He took them in his long, strange arms and devoured them like a mantis picking apart its prey. His mandibles scraped the pieces of meat that hung from his fangs and the bones in the meat splintered under the strength of his jaws.

"Meat," he cried out while spattering blood from his mouth. "More. Meat. Now."

He turned toward her and lunged forward, wrapping his grotesque spikey arms around her and pulling her toward his blood-soaked mouth. She screamed and instinctively covered her head with her arms.

"More. Meat. You. Meat," he said while opening his mouth wider, surrounding her with his foul, hot breath.

"No, Kenneth," she pleaded. "I'm pregnant. Let go of me."

He loosened his grip and peered down at her plump stomach. He carefully scraped his claw across it and tapped the taught skin rapidly with his antennae. "Yes. Spawn. Not. Meat." He flung her towards the door and she slammed into the frame with her shoulder. "More. Different. Meat. Now," he roared at her and clicked his mandibles rapidly. She quickly stepped out into the kitchen and shut the door forcefully behind her.

"Meat. Meat," he kept angrily calling with his mouth full.

She walked through the kitchen and wept, clutching her shoulder with her other arm. She could feel her stomach shifting inside and she felt nauseous. Kenneth banged on the door in rhythmic heaves.

Charles came running from the noise and Jill held out her arms to stop him.

"Come on Charles, let's go back to bed. Your father is still not feeling well." She took his hand and led him away.

They laid on his bed together and once again she touched his hair. Earwigs crawled across her knuckles; some taking shelter in Charles' hair.

Tears welled up in his eyes and he said, "Mommy, I don't like them. I want them to go away." A tear streamed down his cheek and dotted his pillowcase.

"I know honey, but there's nothing we can do about it. There are too many of them. We can learn to live with them. We just have to keep going, okay?"

He sniffled and nodded. "Mommy, your tummy is big."

"That's right. You're going to have a baby brother or sister."

"I am?" he asked and smiled.

"Yes."

"When?"

She paused for a few seconds. "Can't be long now." she said monotonously. After a while, they both fell asleep.

Several hours later, Jill awoke to her stomach rumbling and her throat felt acidic. She got out of bed and hobbled to the bathroom, clutching her enormous stomach as she went. She shut the bathroom door behind her.

She sat on the cold, white, tiled floor next to the toilet, resting one arm on the seat in case she had to throw up. She held her stomach with the other, which swelled like one that was nine months ripe. She felt more movement beneath the taut skin.

She remembered Charles' kicks; little gentle thumps against her skin, but this felt different. The motion was constant, almost like her stomach was growling. She realized her underwear felt wet. She checked and found she was losing blood. She turned white as a sheet and fell unconscious, collapsing onto the cold tile.

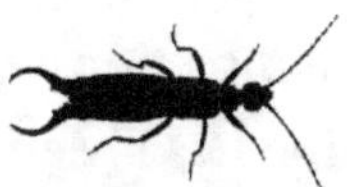

Charles slept through the night. He woke from the sunshine coming through his bedroom window. He walked across the dingy brown carpet which was lined with dead earwigs and live ones climbing over their bodies. He opened the door into the living room and called for his mother, but there was no answer. He thought of checking the bedroom, but remembered his promise to his mother.

He walked to the bathroom door and knocked. There was no answer. He went into the kitchen and poured himself a bowl of Sugar Cones. He climbed onto one of the tall stools at the kitchen counter to eat. He took a few bites, but felt compelled to keep searching for his mother.

Charles set the spoon down in the bowl. Earwigs that had been hiding in the cavernous sugary cones floated up to the surface of the milk. They struggled to save themselves from being drowned and clung to the spoon with their clawed limbs. He stared down at them and wondered why they tried so hard to survive when there were so many of them.

Charles climbed down from his stool and walked back to the bathroom door. "Mommy?" he asked. There was no sound. He turned the knob and the door creaked open. He looked down and saw her lying on the floor. Her arms and legs were small and darkened like the skin of a dried up mummy. He couldn't see her face because her hair laid overtop it. Rising out of her stomach was a white, rounded tower standing four feet high. It had small bumps across its alien surface, and strings of slime branched from it to the ground in all directions.

Charles started breathing heavily and tears pooled in his eyes. He took a few small steps into the room and his curiosity overtook him. He reached his arm out and extended his pointer finger, brushing it against the surface of the bizarre structure.

His tiny finger broke through the wall, which felt like thin, crunchy papier-mâché. A strange smell came from the breach, like a metallic sugary smell that he had never encountered. He covered his nose when a small white insect peeked over the edge of the hole and stood along the wall. Its body was shiny and wet, and it had small, featureless, black eyes. Charles took a cautious step backwards as a few emerged from the opening and climbed along the outside of the egg sac.

Suddenly, a wave of them rushed out of the hole, flowing down the sides like foam dripping down a glass. They poured out onto the floor in a squirming mass as Charles took a few more steps toward the door. Instead of coming toward him, they rushed in the opposite direction and crawled under the door connected to the master bedroom.

Charles stepped out of the bathroom and quietly shut the door. He walked into the kitchen and couldn't help but sob. He knew his mother was gone. He walked over to the stool and kicked it with all his strength. It tipped over and fell to the floor. Charles covered his eyes and wept.

The sudden movement awoke the fat, gray earwig that had been latched to the underside of the stool. It lazily uncurled and started flicking its antennae through the air for its aggressor. Then the phone started ringing. The insect released its grip and rolled onto the ground as Charles walked over to pick up the phone. The gray earwig crawled sluggishly toward the loud ringing sound. He lifted the receiver off the base.

"Hello?"

"Hello, this is Detective Goslin. Are your parents home, son?"

The boy didn't know how to answer.

"I know your father hasn't been at work, is he there?"

"He's sick."

"Can I speak to him?"

"I can't go in there," the boy said while twisting the long phone cord around his finger.

"Can you put your mother on?"

"She's not here," he said and took a step backward. His foot landed on the squishy caterpillar-like body of the gray earwig. It responded by attacking his shoe, wrapping around it like a serpent as it dug its fangs into the hard rubber on the sole.

Charles screamed and dropped the phone, then ran into the living room. The gray earwig pulled his shoe off and writhed around the kitchen floor with it. It skewered the shoe with its pincer tail, and brown liquid oozed from the prongs. The handset hung from its receptacle and swung back and forth from its cord like a pendulum.

Charles watched the gray earwig attacking his shoe from the living room. He crawled onto the counter between them and threw his bowl of cereal at it. It flailed in the milk, but wasn't injured. He realized he needed something bigger. He slid further down the counter and pushed the microwave with all his might. It tipped off of the counter and caught itself on its cord, hanging against the edge of the counter. The creature inched closer towards Charles, sliding through the milk like a snake. Charles tugged on the power cord frantically.

The plug came loose from the wall outlet and crashed to the floor, pinching the gray earwig's upper sections to the ground. It lifted its abdomen into the air, aggressively closing and opening its pincers. It hissed in agony as it died, and yellow goo pooled into the spilled milk on the kitchen floor.

Charles climbed down from the counter, sat on the floor and caught his breath. He watched the slain insect's legs still twitching. Then he heard something stirring beyond the master bedroom door behind him.

"Meat," Kenneth's voice boomed from behind the bedroom door.

Charles climbed down from the kitchen and walked over to the door. "Daddy?" he asked.

"Meat," his father said angrily. "You. Meat."

Charles pressed his ear to the door and repeated, "Daddy?"

Two long black antennae slithered out from under the door and flicked against his shins. They gently cupped the boy's leg and rattled upon feeling the warmth of his body.

"You. Meat," he said between clicking sounds.

Charles fell to the ground in sheer terror and crawled backwards across the kitchen floor. The antennae squeezed his leg so hard it hurt. He grabbed his shoe from the floor nearby and smashed it into the antennae, freeing himself.

The antennae slipped back under the door. "Meat," Kenneth screamed and slammed himself into the door over and over again, cracking the door frame. "Meat!" he roared after each impact.

Charles turned and opened the back door as he heard the bedroom door break into splintered wood behind him. He ran through the backyard towards the forest as fast as he could. Halfway across the yard, he stumbled. He couldn't keep his legs under him and fell, crashing through the dirt and fallen leaves before coming to a stop.

"Son!" a voice behind him called out. The boy stopped and turned around to see Detective Frank Goslin walking through the chain link gate from the front yard. He had his 1911 pistol drawn and jogged towards him.

Charles pointed at the door behind him; too panicked to speak. Frank turned to the sound of the wood breaking inside and walked backwards towards the boy. The creature slid out of the back door into the yard, skidding through the brown leaves that had piled up. It turned to look at the detective with blood red insect eyes.

He was unrecognizable as a human. His entire body had turned to shiny black exoskeleton. His six appendages were a sickly, pale yellow color, and his thorax was long and reddish-brown. Along the creature's back and shoulders were thousands of white earwig children clinging to their father.

Detective Goslin said, "What the hell is that thing?" and aimed his pistol. The creature screeched and began slithering across the ground toward him with alarming speed, kicking dust and leaves into the air. He fired three rounds into the creature before it barreled through the shrubs lining the side of the yard and fled past them into the forest.

Charles ran to the detective who bent down to catch him in his arms.

"It's alright boy, I've got you. What was that thing?"

"That was my father," he said between sobs. "He's a monster."

The detective thought for a moment and said, "Where is your mother?"

"She's in the bathroom."

The detective stood and ran into the house. He knocked on the bathroom door and called her name. When no one answered, he opened the door and saw the consumed body, sucked of all its fluid by the nymphs. He walked out of the house into the backyard again. Charles was crouched next to the cement stairs, shivering. The detective took off his overcoat and put it around him.

"Stay here, boy. More police will be here soon. I'll be back," he said.

The detective entered the forest with his pistol drawn. He walked carefully along the trail the creature made while fleeing. The rows of piled dirt and broken sticks were dotted with drips of yellow liquid. He followed it to the base of towering blue spruce. Its branches formed a dome-like shelter against its trunk. He parted the branches, careful not to poke himself with the sharp blue needles, and saw the creature curled around its base. It was gravely wounded, but he saw the faint lifting and falling of breathing.

"Kenneth?" he asked while keeping his pistol trained on the creature.

The creature reacted to the noise and slowly turned to face the detective. One of his antennae lazily searched through the air, feeling the pine branches around him.

"What happened to your wife? Did you kill her, Kenneth?" the detective asked.

The creature's face changed to something like sorrow as it remembered Jill. Then it emitted horrendous scraping clicks from its mouth. The detective thought it might be weeping. It suddenly stretched towards him in a desperate attack, lunging at the detective's neck. Frank squeezed the trigger, putting a round clean through its head. The creature rolled on its side, its six legs twitching slightly as its grotesque cerci mindlessly pinched the tree trunk.

Soon after, its appendages were still and the creature's breathing stopped. The detective holstered his pistol on his hip and climbed out of the spiky branch shelter. He turned to walk away, not noticing the small, white earwig nymphs crawling up the bark of the trees and through the underbrush all around him.

Frank walked back to find another detective crouching next to Charles. After squinting strenuously, he saw that it was his partner. He was younger than Frank by thirty years and looked spooked. "Nice of you to show up, Ben. Call for some backup," he said.

"Sure boss. Hey, did you get the bastard?"

"I put him down. He's under a tree over yonder. That's a wrap."

Frank walked over to Charles and hoisted the boy off the ground and carried him in his arms. "Come on son, let's get you out of here," he said and walked down the sidewalk. He opened the rear door to his police car and put Charles there. "You'll be safe in here. I have some work to do but it won't take long."

Charles nodded and wiped tears from his face.

A few hours later, the house was taped off and full of officers. Neighbors wrapped in scarves and winter coats gathered around and gossiped. Snowflakes drifted solemnly through the air and dotted the wet ground. Detective Goslin stood on the porch with his partner. They both smoked cigarettes and had the collars on their jackets popped around their necks. They watched as the creature, wrapped in black plastic and strapped to a gurney, was wheeled around the side of the house out to a van on the street.

At that moment, a man from the laboratory at CSU walked out of the house. He was a short man in an overcoat and derby, and wore round framed glasses.

"Well boys, never seen anything like it," he spoke quickly with excitement. "The one we have at the lab is a new species, and the big one you shot is a hybrid. The empty egg-sac on the deceased woman indicates the hybrid successfully reproduced. DNA from one species, blended with another, and a new species was created."

"You think they're out there?" the detective asked.

"Absolutely, we saw evidence that he was carrying the young nymphs on his back. They're probably scattered everywhere in the woods. If they survive the winter, we may have a serious problem on our hands. Not just in this town, but humanity itself could be threatened."

"How d'ya figure?" the young officer asked.

"They eat people, and, by the look of that egg sac, they lay about a hundred eggs per clutch. They could overrun the U.S. in a matter of years."

"What do you suggest we do?" Frank asked.

The scientist thought for a moment and said, "Call in the National Guard, quarantine the whole area, and burn them out. The forest and all the houses in the area."

"I doubt we'd be able to remove these folks from their homes," Frank said.

"Well, I always knew it'd be the bureaucracy that killed us. I've got what I need. Good evening, officers." He tipped his hat and walked down the stone path towards the street.

Ben called out after him, "Sir, before you go, what do you think caused the hybrid? Just a freak mutation?"

The scientist turned around and faced them. "No, it was too specific...too perfect. It had to be genetically engineered. Humans couldn't do this if they tried." He pointed straight up at the sky.

"Aliens?" Ben asked. "You really believe in that hogwash?"

"I didn't, until today. If you ask me, they are the most likely culprits. As for the reason they did it, maybe they don't have one. If they think they are superior to us...well, tell me the last time you thought twice about squashing a bug." He turned and continued down the path towards his car.

The officers sat in silence for a few moments as they blew plumes of smoke into the winter night.

"Well, I think we got the whole story, Ben," Detective Goslin said while taking another drag. "As unbelievable as it is."

"I reckon so, Frank. What the hell kind of world is this where now we have to worry about giant insect creatures?"

"Nothin' new, far as I see it."

"What do you mean?" Ben asked.

"Mr. Chandler was a murderer, same as the ones we got locked up in the jail," he said hoarsely. He took a drag from the cigarette and peered across the street at nothing in particular.

"That thing was more evil than any man I've ever seen."

"More evil than the Boston Strangler? The Zodiac Killer? Don't be naive, Ben. Earwigs are scavengers. They don't kill their own. They don't hunt, they eat dead leaves. They aren't predators."

"What're you getting' at?"

"The evil parts of that thing came from the human side of it." He took a long drag and exhaled a white plume into the frigid air that floated high into the bare branches above them before dissipating into the endless dark. "A certain type of man can become violently unhinged for seemingly no reason at all...when he feels he's lost all control and there is no hope of living a normal life. That's what happened here, same old story."

"Always the pessimist," the younger detective said.

"Can you blame me?"

"I reckon not." Ben paused in thought. "What do we do about the kid?"

Frank looked over at the car. Snow had started to pile up on the windshield.

"I think it's time I up and retired," Frank said. He smiled and slapped Ben on the shoulder. "You've been a great partner, Ben. I know you'll do good work here trying to clean up this town."

"Gee, thanks Frank," he smiled. "Thanks for being the best mentor I could ever hope for."

"The kid can come with me. I'll look after him. I've been dyin' of loneliness lately anyways."

Frank shook his partner's hand one last time and walked to his police car, carefully climbed into the driver's seat, and closed the door.

"Sorry for the wait, son," Frank said.

"That's okay, mister," Charles said.

"What do you say we get outta here? Go someplace far away. Somewhere warm, near the ocean. Sound good?"

Charles nodded.

Frank put the car into gear and pulled away as "Going Up The Country" by Canned Heat played on the radio.

Overhead, above the tall maples lining the street, the three rotating red lights noiselessly drifted away, climbing high into the brooding clouds.

The End

The End

She was wrapped in a towel, standing in her bathroom, thoroughly applying her foundation. Finishing the final touches of the base application, she closed her eyes in thought. The show the previous day had been jarring enough. She never liked it when minors were on. She knew their sadness was real, she could see it in their eyes. She felt anxious when she realized the gravitas of the upcoming show. It made her nervous to think of how many people would be watching.

General McMillan sent her the encoded message at four o'clock in the morning: they had captured a terrorist by the name of Michael Grad. McMillan's team had been pursuing Grad for eleven weeks, ever since he attacked an office building in Michigan with an assault weapon, but he escaped instead of taking his own life. The media didn't cover the story until military intelligence branded him a terrorist, confirming that he was conspiring to bring down the government. The story had been all over the news. There was only one punishment for treason; it was a supreme offense.

She began the task of drying and straightening her long, white-blonde hair and putting the rest of her makeup on. She wanted things to look just right; she knew there would be millions watching. She dressed in her executioner's gear: the base layer was a skintight black jumpsuit, the outer was a large crimson hood that covered her face in shadows and flowed into a long cloak that extended to her calves. The cloak's design was influenced by the longest running executioner in the Papal States of old: nicknamed Mastro Titta–Master of Justice. Fastened to her shoulders were flared silver pauldrons, and on her torso, a silver fitted breastplate matched with purple-tinted metal vambraces and greaves.

The outfit was more of a symbol of her power than of actual defensive use in combat. Her 'patients' were always unarmed and shackled. They were cowardly, pitiful excuses for human beings. However, she was commissioned to wear the ensemble and didn't care enough to alter its design. Besides, she looked fierce, she thought as she smeared dark purple makeup over both eyes in a wide band across her face. She opened her bright blue eyes and stared at herself in the mirror. She smiled sinisterly, then spun and walked out into the hallway.

Hanging from a loop holster at her side was her plasma ax she named 'Ker'. The hilt could be glimpsed when her long crimson cloak would flow in the wind as she walked. It had a golden handle and a platinum ax head, with plasma coils running along the bladed edge in illuminated pink lines. She had single-handedly struck down over six thousand criminals with Ker, which was twelve times as many patients as Mastro Titta killed in his lengthy career. Her justices were televised, and none of her patients ever required a second swing. Her silver boots clacked loudly on the polished stone flooring as she walked past two guards into the elevator.

"The Justice Floor please", she spoke aloud.

The elevator chimed and zipped upwards, stopping at the 95th floor. She lived and worked in the Capitol Building along with the rest of the administration, which was a requirement of the position. The General's team kept a watchful eye on everyone to ensure any assassination attempts would be faltered. She entered into an antechamber where a few people in suits greeted her and checked her armor to make sure everything was in order. A few straps were adjusted to make the armor fit tighter. A makeup artist gave her a quick once-over and nodded in approval. The host could be heard in the studio ahead as his voice boomed through the speakers for the live audience in the main room.

Tapping the side of her headset, one of the suits said "She is here."

The suit fastened a small mic to the cloak above her chest before smiling. "Okay you're green, go ahead and go out there when he calls you. You know the drill."

On the stage, the host stood with his hands clasped together in front of him. He wore a black tuxedo and a flashy smile, his voice emanated energy and charisma through the room.

"My good people!" the host exclaimed. "It is time to begin so quiet down a little...try to contain yourselves if you can...for we have a worthy purpose to fulfill! We are here to make sure that those in our society that are unclean, those that are vile, horrible, insatiable, unholy cretins, are brought to justice." Adjusting his wide Double Windsor knot in his red neck tie, the host smiled. "These disgusting people", he said as he swept his arms towards the three men sitting behind him on stage with red hoods over their heads, "are such people! They will be brought to justice for conspiring against our government. For conspiring against the citizens of the United Order of America!" He turned towards a balcony seat on the right side of the grand auditorium and extended his arm towards the man who was sitting there. The man had white-blonde hair surrounding his baldness and wore a black suit jacket with navy suit pants.

The host continued, "For conspiring against our leader! The Anointed One is unmatched in his wisdom and all-knowing clarity, isn't he folks? Take a bow sir! Your resilience and bravery are admirable!" The crowd erupted in applause as the Anointed One struggled to get out of his seat. Once standing, he smirked proudly, took a bow, and mouthed "thank you" to the crowd. Then he flopped into his chair and tried to catch his breath.

"Now, everyone: Listen", the announcer continued, "you know who we got to come out to dispatch these unholy demons? We only bring the best! That is why we brought out the chief executioner for today. The crimson angel that flies on swift wings to end the lives of all who are evil. The queen of merciful retribution! You love her, I love her, ladies and gentlemen: The End!"

The crowd cheered as The End walked out onto the stage, stopping next to the men sitting in the chairs. They shifted nervously in their seats, pulling on their restraints, and would have screamed out loud if they weren't muzzled beneath their hoods. She waved at the crowd and blew kisses. Then she put her hand on her hip, pulling back her cloak to reveal the golden handle of Ker, which made the crowd explode into a deafening roar.

"That's right folks, shhh shhh. I know. She is a force unknown to the natural world. Empowered by the Anointed One to remove those demons that live among us. Blessed with the touch of death. These three devils up on the stage today have all broken the Articles of Ascension. The first one killed thirty four people in an office building to which he wasn't acquainted. This random act of violence must be punished with utmost severity. The other two were not his accomplices, but they have chosen to live their lives in sin, against the supreme culture in which we choose to live. The one in the middle chose to live in filth of the body as a gold-duster. The last one lived in filth of the mind and has chosen to remain a devout Muslim."

The host walked over to the strange, glistening metal tablets that were on display atop a white marble column on the side of the stage. They both had rows of articles inscribed into them. He placed his hand atop them.

"Thank the Anointed One for enforcing these laws of infinite wisdom in order to purify our society, and for protecting us against threats to our lives." The host turned toward The End and bowed. "My dear, if you would be so kind."

She slowly pulled back the red hood of the first man and recognized Grad's face. He was sniveling and had blue eyes that were bloodshot from tears. Sweat ran from the top of his head. His short brown hair was disheveled and messy. The End grabbed the handle of her ax and pulled it out, using a flick of her wrist to extend the handle several feet. The ax powered on, coating the gleaming silver blade in an arc of neon pink plasma, which cackled loudly as it superheated the air around it.

She cleared her throat and spoke with infallible determination, "Through your actions you have been condemned to execution. I am The End, and the last thing you will feel is the bite of Ker before I claim your life for The United Order of America. With your death, the planet grows stronger." She brought the ax above her right shoulder then spun it over so the long spike on the back of the ax faced toward him, then brought it abruptly downward on her victim. The spike hit clean and pierced the top of Grad's head. She lifted the spike out of it which limply fell backwards in the chair and spilled blood onto the floor. The End turned and faced the crowd, hoisting Ker into the air in victory. The crowd proudly chanted her name in repetitious harmony with the vigor of a people united under the glory of the Anointed One.

She turned and yanked the hood off of the next criminal. It was a man she had never seen before, but the sight of his face made her angry. He glanced over to Grad. At the sight of his corpse, the man panicked and flailed against his restraints. His eyes pleaded with her, stared into the shadows beneath her hood, hoping for mercy.

"Have you been practicing this face you are making? Trying to look innocent? Pathetic duster," she said slyly, then raised her ax above her head with both hands, bringing it down with thundering force on the top of his head. The attack cleaved the man in half and Ker crashed into the floor, cracking the black stone beneath them. The crowd cheered again at the amazing display of ruthless power.

The End pulled her ax across the ground and hefted it over her right shoulder. With her left hand she pulled back the hood of the last criminal, who shook violently from fear.

"What do we have here? Do you see what happened to your friends?" she asked. The man looked at the carnage next to him and lost consciousness.

"Oh look at that," she said, turning to face the audience. "I guess I scared him!" She shrugged and pouted her bottom lip in innocence. Two suits ran out and touched a soft, gold colored powder to the criminal's nose, and he instantly was fully awake again. The End spun to face him. "There you are again!" she yelled. Then she held her ax up to his face and slowly let the plasma cut through it, letting the weight of the ax head gradually slice through to the other side of his skull as smoke poured out of the gash. The top of his skull dropped off and fell to the floor of the studio.

She spun around and thrust her ax up into the air repeatedly while the crowd cheered, then deactivated the plasma blade, collapsed the handle, and sheathed it. The announcer strolled back onto the stage and boomed, "Let's hear it for The End everyone! No one does it better!" The End bowed several times and waved to her adoring fans.

"Don't go away folks! We aren't quite done here. Some justice remains to be served, is that right my dear?" the host asked.

"That's right," The End said to the crowd. "For the unforgivable, unimaginable acts that Michael Grad has committed, I am tasked with quartering him. I have killed the man, but now I must kill his soul. To the Stone of Banishing!"

The crowd cheered excitedly. She walked over and released Michael's restraints, then carried him over her shoulder. She marched to the elevator as the camera crew followed her, leaving a trail of blood in her wake.

"To Heaven's Reach," she spoke as the elevator climbed to the roof.

She walked into the misting rain onto the rooftop with the camera crew exiting after her and getting in position to film. In the middle of the rooftop was a flat, gray, polished stone, stained red from blood that the rain hadn't washed away. She approached the stone and slumped the body onto it, laying him onto his back. She fastened clasps to his limp wrists and ankles. Chains ran from the clasps outward in all four directions. At the end of each one was a harness attached to an enormous mechanized horse. All four of them were dull and tarnished, but had glowing eyes embedded into their metal heads that stared at the body she laid before them. The horses pawed the gravel beneath them in anticipation.

"Pestilence, Death, War, Famine. I call upon each of you to punish this sinner. He will not be named here, for one's such as him do not carry a name beyond death. It is his soul you must destroy, to ensure he does not return on this planet or anywhere else. By the power imbued in me by the Anointed One, I command it."

The horses turned from the center in perfect synchronicity and reared back on their hind legs. Their rusted hooves carved at the ground as they lurched into a gallop. They leapt forward upon reaching the end of their leads. A flash of lightning illuminated them for a split second as they slammed against the chains, tearing Grad's body completely apart. The stone was splashed with a fresh coat of red. Shimmering raindrops pattered onto the stone, streaking the blood down its sides.

"With that, the patient is banished," The End said with a camera in her face.

The suit signaled: 3...2...1...cut. "We got it. That was amazing! Let's get you back inside and out of this rain."

That evening there was a celebration held at the Prince George Ballroom. It was one of the most luxurious ballrooms in New York, and a frequent reception hall for the administration. The End was supposed to attend, but she didn't feel like dealing with the public praise. She sat on a black velvet couch in the living room of her flat, waiting for her neon yellow nail polish to dry. Lightning flashed outside her window, but the light was dimmed from the oily, black rain that streaked down the glass.

She scrolled through the contacts on her citizen device, trying to decide who she should bring as a date. After doing some comparisons in her head, she decided to see if Kevin Walcott was available. Kevin had starred in the summer's biggest movie, "The Cleanser", which was about a man hired by the government to assassinate the leader of a terrorist organization.

She laughed thinking about how he was basically playing the male version of her, but his character was more of a secret agent than an executioner. She hadn't gone on a mission since her Future War tour ended six years prior. Now the criminals were brought to her and she ended them. She preferred it that way.

Kevin was a douchebag pretty boy and dumb as a bag of rocks, but he would be good arm candy for the night. She messaged him asking him if he was free for the evening.

"Anything for you, E," he replied.

He picked her up on the waterway outside the Capitol Building in the latest Chiron superboat. It was painted silver with deep blue racing stripes and was so loud she had to cover her ears. She could see his white teeth shining through the boat's window as she approached it. The doorman opened the butterfly door for her and she stepped into the closed cabin, collapsed her umbrella, and set it under her seat.

"Damn, E. You look amazing, really," he said in a low voice as he stared at her. She was wearing a black dress with silver sparkles that faded out from the bottom. Long black feathers came off of her shoulders and back, and she wore a silver eye mask that was sprouting black and purple feathers. Her blonde hair was long and straight past her shoulders.

The man closed the door and she smiled at Kevin. He looked clean cut, with short brown hair styled up, light blue eyes, and a broad grin showing his perfect white smile. She thought of Michal Grad's hair and the spike she put through it for a moment but tried to get the image out of her head. She reached over and touched his shoulder with her gloved hand and said, "Thanks Kevin. You're looking sharp in the tux as well."

"It's party time," he said as he slammed the boat into gear and revved the engine loudly. The four propellers spun rapidly, spraying water behind the boat and launching them down the waterway. Kevin was a show-off, but she had to admit: he did make her heart swell at times. They sped through the dark, murky waterways of the city, completely untouchable by the law.

Side traffic began to cross a red light intersection, making Kevin curse and bring the boat to a stop. The End looked out the window and watched the sidewalks rise and fall with the waves caused by the boat traffic. The floating walkways had been installed around the perimeter of every building back when the ocean first moved into the city, to accommodate the tides. Floating trash was heaped against them, pushed to the side by the boat traffic, and the city's reigning pests, aquatic junker beetles, clumsily navigated their mountainous homes. Covering the garbage and climbing up the side of the buildings was the beetle's food; the vibrant purple algae that survived off of the aquatic waste. It faintly glowed from bioluminescence, casting a haunting purple light upon the water.

She saw people scuttling on walkways with their umbrellas. Looking down an alleyway, something caught her eye. A woman was slumped against the wall with her young daughter sitting next to her, basking in the yellow light cast by the exterior light fixture above them. The sounds of the superboat's engine made the girl look over at them and notice the beautiful watercraft. She tugged on her mother's shirt and pointed at them. The mother lazily looked over and stared at her. Recognizing The End, the mother jumped and her mouth dropped open in reverence.

One of the many patrolling UOA officers, commonly called flatcaps on account of the myriad of scanning tech installed into their circular helmets, was walking down the walkway towards them. The flatcap's helmets looked similar to sandogasa hats that Ronin warriors used to wear, but instead of being woven from straw they were made of slick matte-black metal. It was more of a helmet than a hat, covering their eyes completely, stopping just above their exposed mouths. Along the front face of the helmet were four orange lenses that scanned targets and displayed their information instantly within the helmet. The flatcaps also shared the mercenary sensibilities of the Ronin, capturing or killing any-one on the streets they could find that the UO wanted brought in. The grayish rain was caught by the helmet and shed away from the officer as he walked toward them.

The flatcap noticed the woman staring at The End, and his four sensors glowed orange. He called out at them and aimed his standard-issue rifle at the woman and child. The little girl jumped to her feet and ran down the alleyway. The mother hurried after her. The flatcap lowered his weapon, spun to face The End and saluted her. She nodded and smiled at the officer. He turned and went about his patrol.

"Why do these people choose to live like this on the street? With children too," The End asked.

"They like living with the junker beetles, I guess. These filthy dusters would rather shoot up than give their kid a chance," Kevin responded.

"I wish we could do something to make them stop. Make them be normal. Why would anyone want to take gold dust anyways?"

"My dear, you are already doing all that you can. You scare people into behaving. Some people...they'd rather choose death." Kevin said as he floored it through the green light, splashing water on a few pedestrians in his rush.

The End laughed and said "To what end though? If we executed all the dusters in this city, would there even be anyone left?"

"Only those worthy of living, my dear," he said with a wink.

They continued slicing through the dark water until they arrived at the ballroom. Her butterfly door swung open and she was immediately bathed in bright camera flashes. Kevin took her arm and walked along the dock toward the entrance. The building was magnificently decorated in banners from the administration, proudly displaying the flag of the United Order of America: a blue rectangle with a white hand pointing skywards in the upper left corner, and the red and white stripes of the old colonies.

Inside there were scores of wealthy politicians and their plastic wives talking loudly in groups throughout the hall. There was a plethora of food, with waiters gliding around to serve people. Wide, black banners hung from the ceiling, and an orchestra in the corner filled the stuffy air with pleasant music of old. The End quickly grabbed a cocktail and drank half of it in one gulp.

"Getting a head start on me E?" Kevin asked as he sipped his martini and looked dashingly off into the distance.

The End almost laughed at the face he was making but she contained herself. "Sorry, it was a hard day," she said while looking down.

He dramatically turned toward her and spoke with concern, "I can only imagine how much pressure you were under, taking care of that guy today. But you did a great job. You really are the best at what you do."

"Thanks Kev. You're pretty good at what you do, too."

Kevin puffed his chest out, smiled broadly and said, "If you could go ahead and tell that to the academy that would be swell. They would probably give me an Oscar out of fear alone."

The End laughed and grabbed Kevin's hand to hold.

He looked down at her hand and said, "So cold, like touching death herself."

She smiled at him. Her gaze drifted across the room until it landed on the Anointed One. He was sitting on a vibrant golden throne, looking like he was asleep or was about to be, with his typical following of strumpets at his side. She couldn't imagine why any of them would want to marry the man.

Beside him were two of the highest ranking flatcap body-guards, and behind him was the famed General, showering him with compliments and sharing champagne with him. The End finished the rest of her drink.

The Anointed One sat lazily, squinting at the guests as they arrived. His fat lips were permanently pursed, and he wore a tall ceremonial hat to cover his bald, liver-spotted head. She was disgusted by the sight of him and had to look away. Even though he was the leader of the world and had been chosen to bring the planet under a single flag, she despised him on a personal level.

The End didn't remember much from the time before the Anointed One was chosen to lead the world. She was only six years old at the time, but her father was the one who put her on the path to become the head executioner for the government. He had taken a liking to her early on as her father was exposing her to the administration. Her father knew that in the new world, those who were on top would have the greatest chance of survival. Humanity wasn't going to like the answers they were given, but when the answers were true, indisputably so, they would be forced to comply. Gaining the favor of the Anointed One at any cost became the only thing that mattered. Her father was right of course, she would rather be a high-ranking official in the government than living in the slums with most of the population, and she was grateful for the position she had ascended to.

But something felt wrong about the Anointed One. She felt it deep inside when she first started working for the administration. The way he behaved was bizarre, and she hated his rambling, incoherent speeches that had little to do with the problems facing the world. He barely ever moved, and was toted about on his throne by his elite guards. Despite his obesity, he never seemed to eat. Suddenly as she was watching him, he glanced over and met her gaze, squinting at her through his saggy eyelids.

Kevin suddenly pulled his hand away and said, "Ay-ay-ay! Ease up that grip a little, E."

She looked at him with tears pooling in her big blue eyes. She quickly wiped them away and said, "It's nothing Kev. Sorry about your hand." He stared at her with a confused and concerned look, thinking of something to say. Her face was red with embarrassment and she said, "I'm just gonna go to the ladies room. I'll be back in a minute."

As she was reapplying her eye shadow in the wide bathroom mirror, a woman walked in and stopped at the sink next to her. She noticed the short, dark-skinned woman, who appeared to be in her fifties and wore a green silk dress, was staring at her through the reflection. The End stared back at her, and noticed that the woman was visibly upset. The stranger was looking at her with her pleading, green eyes and said, "I have information about the man you murdered this morning. I think you want to hear it. Meet me at Hudson River Park tonight." Then she grabbed her purse off of the sink and quickly walked out of the bathroom.

The End finished applying her makeup, trying to process what had happened. Calling her a murderer was a supreme offense against the United Order. The stranger could be charged with treason. The End could have killed the woman right there, but something in her eyes showed her conviction. She fully believed The End committed murder. The woman's eyes had told her that she didn't care if she was killed right where she stood. The End keyed in a message on her citizen device: **Need your help. Wait above Prince George Ballroom for pickup.** She sent the message and walked out of the bathroom into the main hall.

The evening continued with a congratulatory ceremony praising the Anointed One for foiling another plot to overthrow him. Then they told the story about how the Anointed One was chosen to lead humanity towards the future. How the spacecraft had landed on the White House lawn, and the Enlightened One emerged and spoke with the then-President of the United States.

In this meeting, the Enlightened One told the President that he had been chosen to bring humanity together as a single species, that he was the obvious choice out of all of the leaders on Earth. The Enlightened One also gave him the famed Articles of Ascension that were later drafted and set as rule of law. These were to be the guidelines that all humans would live by if we were going to prosper as a species. For anyone to deny them meant they would be killed. This was the only way to be truly unified.

Included in them was the article requiring that a head executioner would be appointed to quell those who refused to follow the path to ascension; those who would hold our entire species back from progressing. After the retelling of the rise of the Anointed One, The End was brought up on stage and thanked for destroying the most recent conspirator and the other impurities of society. She smiled and waved, but her thoughts were about the mysterious meeting that night.

Afterwards she met with Kevin again and told him it was time for her to leave. They walked out of the ballroom into the cold New York air and stopped on the stairs leading to the entrance. The sounds of the splashing waterways and boat horns echoing off the buildings filled the air.

"Are you ready to go home?" Kevin asked.

"I'm not heading home yet, Kev. I've got some work to do tonight", she said, moving her mouth to one side.

Kevin dropped his shoulders and said, "Dang, I was hoping to maybe get lucky with The End." He looked up at her with soft eyes and smiled.

She smiled back and said, "In your dreams, Kev. Gotta run!" She was encased in a ghostly, blue light that faded in with a flash, then disappeared. Kevin looked up and saw the faint outline of the aircraft she was transported to hovering about a hundred feet overhead. He opened his umbrella and walked down the dock toward his boat.

The End stepped off of the transport pad into the hull of the ship. It was a standard recon ship that was about eighty feet long. The interior was a dark olive color and mainly metal aside from the padded seating along both walls of the interior. Lines of lights ran along the edges of the ceiling, dimly lighting the cabin, and the smell of gasoline faintly filled the air. There were also benches and a gaming table towards the cockpit for the crew to eat on longer flights, and a bathroom and changing room in the rear of the ship. The engines could still be heard in a low hum from their position on both wings.

Three members of her old Special Forces team were there. Gunther was the stern pilot up in the cockpit that didn't look back. Alice "Fox" Jenning and Jack "Tommy" Thompson started whooping and whistling mockingly when they saw her dressed up.

"You're seriously going on a mission dressed like that?" Tommy said while wiping his eyes from laughter.

"Hell no, get this pretty dress off of me," The End pleaded.

Fox glared at Tommy. "That's why we brought her armor, genius," she said between gum chews. "I think she looks hot."

The End scowled at Tommy and said, "Watch yourself, Tommy. Even in this outfit I could still kick your ass."

"Maybe...you're all political and shit now," Tommy said through a wide smile.

"It's so good to see you," The End said happily.

Seeing her squad mates again felt great, but they seemed different since their last mission six years ago. Tommy was muscular and wore an army green t-shirt with a black tactical vest over it filled with plasma magazines. A black digital camouflage helmet protected his head, which could convert into full-face cover if he needed visual enhancements. A chain necklace displaying his dog tags hung from his thick dark neck. The wooden handle of his Thompson gun stuck out of his chest holster. The weapon was part of the reason people called him Tommy. He loved the style of the weapon even though it was a design from over a century ago. He modified it himself so it fired accelerated plasma rounds at about three times the original rate of fire. His thick, short beard was now intertwined with white hairs that had invaded the familiar black ones.

The redhead sitting across from him was Fox: a nickname given to her not just for her red hair but also because of her speed and stealth. Her hair was up in long spiraled pigtails, a style she always wore to keep her hair out of her face while looking down a rifle scope. She wore a black skin-tight jumpsuit with built-in stealth systems that was designed to swallow light. The material was so dark that her slender body looked like a silhouette. Her white painted light rifle was always at her side and was the most lethal weapon available. She had used it to claim the record for the most confirmed kills with a single shot: eight unlucky bastards that were dumb enough to open fire at Tommy while taking cover in a line against the same wall. She angled herself at their side and killed them simultaneously with a wide beam shot. The End wasn't sure if she still had the record and wasn't about to risk pissing her off if someone else had taken it.

"So what's the plan? What do we know about the mission?" Fox asked.

"Not much," The End said. "All we have is the location. Something tells me she just wants to talk. But she was hostile towards me, and emotional. So stay frosty."

"Hey you know me," Tommy said while pulling back the receiver on his Thompson and clapping it forward. "I'll go in with you and keep ten meters back. Fox will find a perch to watch over us."

"I'll circle wide and scan the perimeter," the pilot said.

"Thanks Gunther," The End said. "Sounds like a plan."

"Get changed," Fox said while motioning to one of the side compartments in the rear of the ship.

The End took off her magnificent feathered attire and changed into her silver armor and cloak. She held the golden hilt of Ker in her hands, touching the smooth lines etched across its surface. For some reason she felt hesitant to use it. She shook her insecure feelings off and holstered her weapon, then stepped out into the cabin of the ship again.

Tommy smiled wide and said, "There we go! Now my girl is back."

Fox looked her up and down and said, "You look a lot scarier."

"Get ready! We're coming up to the park," Gunther said.

"I'm going to drop on this rooftop, I'll have a clear shot," Fox said while keying in the location on a screen next to the transport pad. She stepped onto the pad and flashed out into blue light and was gone. Tommy and The End walked over to the screen and could see the icon on the map showing where Fox was perched. Tommy keyed in their drop point, towards the end of the park next to the Hudson. They stepped onto the pad and instantly found themselves on the ground.

The air was cold and filled with swirling mist from the waves crashing loudly on the sides of the buildings below the elevated park. A light rain was falling overhead. The End cautiously walked down the path which was lined with ground lights. The glowing blue eyes on Tommy's helmet watched The End every step of the way from the darkness behind her.

"I have eyes on her," Fox said through the radio channel. "She's alone, sitting on a bench about twenty yards straight in front of you."

"Copy," The End replied.

She saw the figure sitting on the bench in a hooded jacket. The park was deserted and behind the sound of the water all around her came the low rumbling of thunder in the clouds above. Echoing throughout the park were the sounds of sirens from within the city, overlaid with the metallic pattering of rainfall on her shoulder pauldrons. There was a sense of uncertainty that surrounded The End, and chills flowed across her skin. She kept her ax sheathed as she walked in a wide circle in order to approach the woman head on.

She stopped several feet in front of the figure sitting on the bench. Aware of The End's presence, the woman looked up.

"You came," she said flatly.

"Who are you?" The End asked.

"I'm not anybody anymore. I didn't have much before, but now—" she shook her head and continued, "You took everything that I had. My husband is gone. You killed him this morning."

"Michael Grad?"

"Not him. The black man next to him was my husband, George Temple. I'm his...widow. Gracie," she said while struggling to keep the emotion out of her soft voice.

The End stood in silence for a while, and then replied, "He was a sinner."

Gracie laughed abruptly and said, "Everyone is, but not in the way that they said. I would know if my husband was shooting gold dust, and believe me, he wouldn't touch the stuff."

"Our judicial system doesn't make mistakes," The End said through clenched teeth.

"I'm not saying it was a mistake. I'm saying it was an intentional, outright lie," Gracie snapped. "Flatcaps broke in and took him away two nights ago and now he's dead. There was no trial, no justice...only a murder."

The End rolled her eyes. "Why would the flatcaps want him to be executed? He must have done something wrong."

"My husband's only crime was finding the truth. People who know what's really going on wind up dead, as I soon will be," she said. Sorrow weighed on her words.

"The truth about what?" The End said while crossing her arms.

"The United Order of America, the Anointed One, the cause of the Future War; the whole state of the world. It's all a ploy to control everything and hoard power," she said.

The End sighed and said, "Another conspiracy theorist. I've heard the same babble before. You think first contact didn't actually happen, yet you have seen the vids. They were tested and confirmed to be real, and thousands of people witnessed it with their own eyes. How can you deny things that are proven to be factual?"

"The footage was real, that can't be disputed. But what it captured was not. The ship was experimental Air Force tech...built by humans, not aliens. You don't think it was strange that the aliens showed up in a flying saucer? It was the most cliché choice they could have made."

"Not if the Enlightened Ones had visited Earth before, to study us, and that's why aliens were always portrayed in that type of craft when people would report sightings."

"That's a stretch."

"It wasn't some stage prop. The design was functional, we all saw it flying. I believe the things that I see. If you questioned empirical evidence you'd never get anything done."

"You didn't see it yourself; you are too young. I was there for it. When it was happening there was this sense of shock and a feeling of obvious doubt. Why would they choose him? He is one of the least intelligent, vile, misogynistic, racist, and greedy leaders that we have ever had. It makes no sense that a higher power would choose him."

"I get it, you didn't vote for him, but the rest of the country did. He was the President of the United States. We had already chosen him to lead us, why wouldn't the Enlightened One do the same?"

"Yeah and it was the biggest mistake this country has ever made. Just look at the billions that have died since then. The Future War that he created to make the world bow to him."

The End took a step toward her and pointed at her, "I fought in the Future War. Their deaths were necessary. They weren't opposing us as a country, they were opposing the future of the planet. They had to die quickly or we'd be stuck in a never-ending war. It was all predicted by the Enlightened One."

Gracie rose to her feet and shouted, "They were right to oppose him! They knew that fat piece of shit was playing them for fools! Erasing their legacies to fill his ego!"

"You have plenty of emotions, but seem to have no proof. It wasn't just a flying saucer. The Enlightened One walked out of it, spoke, and gave us artifacts from space. Lemme guess, that was just a guy in a rubber suit?"

"It sure wasn't an alien being or a human in a costume. It was an animatronic robot designed by researchers at New York Dynamics, a robotics company."

The End took Ker into her hand and activated the blade, coating them both in pink light. "This is bullshit. You can't just make claims like this without anything to back it up. I've heard these ramblings before by conspirators and silenced them myself. You have committed treason." The rain hissed as it fell into the plasma coils and evaporated.

The woman stepped back, started sobbing and said, "You can kill me. I knew that was a risk. But before you do, take this. It's not a weapon. It's the real reason my husband was murdered."

She reached into her jacket and pulled out a small data card, then held it out towards The End. "It's a copy he made that the sweepers missed. See the truth for yourself. Just don't use your citizen device to read it, that's how they caught George."

The End deactivated her ax, stepped forward, took the data card and put it into her pocket.

"I'll look into it. How did this data find its way into George's hands? It seems like such convenient proof would be widely available by now."

She laughed and said, "Not when every piece of data is monitored. Not when every voice is silenced. How do you not know how far his reach is? You've been the one killing all of these people." She lowered her head and looked at the wet pavement, "George might have had plans to distribute it, but he knew anyone he sent it to would be killed too."

"Where did he get it?" The End asked firmly.

The woman stared The End in the eyes and said, "I won't tell you. I won't let any more people be killed."

"I've heard enough," The End said, then turned and walked towards the pier.

Fox's voice came through her earpiece, "Say the word if you want her dead."

"No. She might have more intel. Tommy, take her. Gunther, we need a pick up," The End replied.

"On it," Tommy said as he walked past her towards the bench. The End heard the woman cry out as Tommy put her in restraints, and The End was suddenly standing inside the hull of the ship again. The instant contrast between temperatures was pleasant. Tommy and the prisoner materialized in the hull and he walked her back to a holding cell in the rear of the ship. Fox followed them in and had a somber look on her face.

"Wow. Are these the types of crazies you have to deal with now? I was hoping for some action. What are you gonna do now?" Fox asked.

The End met her gaze and said, "I don't know. For all I know this data card is just going to corrupt any device I load it into. But I still want to know what's on it."

"Aren't you gonna take it to General McMillan's research team?" Fox asked while biting her thumb nail.

"I know that's the protocol, but I need to make absolutely sure this doesn't fall into the wrong hands. Let's not mention the data card to anyone for now, okay?"

Fox stopped biting her nail and said, "I won't mention it."

"Neither will I," Tommy said.

"Thanks," The End said sincerely. "Gunther! Can you drop me at my place? Then you can take the prisoner in for questioning." Gunther gave a thumbs up.

As they traveled to the Capitol Building, The End watched the reflections in the waterways below through a rain streaked window. The city was dark and dead. Few boats were out and fewer people still were walking on the side docks. One could blame it on the rain, but it rained every day for as long as she could remember. The war changed the atmosphere, and though the fighting had mostly stopped a few years prior, the climate was never the same. The Future War kicked up so much ash, soot, and radiation into the air that it refused to settle, creating a thick cloud layer that enveloped the planet.

The administration boasted that crime was down, something that she felt she personally had a hand in, but they also said drug use was at an all-time low. What she saw in the city each night told a different story. She saw the flatcap raids, the blaring sirens, the recon ships flying through the city watching everyone. New York City had become the capital of the new world, and, though the war had effectively ended, it seemed as if no one wanted to live there. She knew about the drug dens that people went to and gave up on everything. They all just wanted to overdose on dust or grab a rifle and take out as many people as they could before ending it all. Those were the specialized jobs that Tommy and Alice had been working since she saw them last.

A tear streamed down her face and she couldn't help but wonder what the world would have been like if the Enlightened One never came to power. She wished she could compare the two, just to see the difference. She felt helpless as she accepted there was no way to change the past. At that moment, the Capitol Building slid into view, looming over the dark city like a tombstone. With a crack of thunder, it lit up in white light for a split second, and then was shrouded in darkness again, bending and changing through the rain on the black glass window.

"Get ready to drop out," Gunther said.

She wiped the tear from her face and walked over to the transport pad.

"I'll keep in touch with you guys. Thanks for everything," she said while tapping the screen.

"Take care of yourself, E," Fox said. In a flash of light The End was gone, transported into her quarters.

The lights turned on after detecting her presence, and the calming, electronic melodies of ambient synthwave started playing. She exhaustedly unbuckled the straps of her armor, piece by piece, until she was in her underwear. She flopped onto her bed and looked up at the ceiling. She held the data card up that Gracie had given her and wondered how to look inside without getting traced. She spun the card between her fingers, imagining the secrets it held. She sat up and turned the device over. She moved it closer to the card slot. As she was about to insert it, her citizen device started ringing. She flipped it back over and saw that General McMillan was calling. She tapped the button to answer it.

"Hey Dad," she said.

"Hello darling," the raspy voice of the general replied. "I heard that you went out hunting today with your old team. Find anything interesting?"

"Not really. The wife of one of the men I executed today wanted to have some words with me. It's happened before. She is being delivered to your team right now."

"Excellent. What should we be looking for?"

"Find out who told her husband all of the ridiculous conspiracy theories she was parroting to me. That's all I need from her. Someone is spreading these rumors and they must be dealt with."

"Understood. Great job today on the show, at the celebration, and on this mission. I'm proud of you."

"I know. Thanks Dad, love you."

"I love you too. I'll let you know what my team finds just as soon as they extract. Talk to you soon."

She hung up and, after placing her citizen device on the nightstand, pulled the soft covers over herself and fell asleep.

A few hours later her device chimed. She awoke and unlocked it. A message from her father was there, it read:

"Found the target. We've been tracking him for a while now. Your prisoner caved easily and told us where he is located. He goes by the alias "Arbiter"; we don't know his real name. Move quickly. He may be cautious if he watched you bring George to justice. Do not let him slip away. I've sent the coordinates. Your team has been notified and they are en route to you now."

She set her device down and sat up, dangling her legs over the edge of her bed. She glanced over at the data card on her nightstand and sighed.

"I'll make the nerd show me what's on it," she said to herself and stood up. She hopped in the shower and watched the oily grime run off her body and swirl into the drain. Washing it off always felt good. She finished, dried herself off, and suited up in a new set of armor that had already been cleaned and polished, then reapplied her trademark purple eye stripe. The transport request came through on her citizen device just as she finished getting ready. She accepted it and was immediately standing in the hold of the ship again.

"Gunther! You have the coordinates?" The End called out.

"You betcha. Departing now," the pilot replied.

The ship's engines roared as it surged forward, and The End grabbed onto one of the leather loops fastened to the ceiling to steady herself.

Tommy and Fox turned toward The End and waited to be briefed.

"Long time no see," Tommy said.

"Sorry to dispatch you guys so soon, but we need to get to the bottom of this quickly, before any sensitive information falls into more of the wrong hands."

Tommy frowned and said, "I didn't get to finish my Chinese food."

"Sorry big guy. I'll take you out when we are all done with this," The End said.

Fox smiled and said, "I didn't kill anyone last time, so that didn't really count as work. What's the plan?"

The End set her device onto the gaming table in the kitchen area, and a topographical map hologram materialized.

"We are going after a hacker that the administration has been after for years. He goes by the alias Arbiter. His identity, age, race, everything is unknown about him. We got a tip from our captive that he was located here in a village in Nova Scotia. The data says he was in contact with... Michael Grad?"

"The mass shooter you executed?" Tommy asked. "How are they connected?"

"I don't know," she said while swiping through the data she was given. "But we are going to find out," The End said.

The map expanded and showed steep mountains surrounding a small town at the center of a large island.

"Looks like we are going to the great white north," Tommy said. "I guess it's more brown now than white. What's our ETA, Gunther?"

"Twenty minutes," he replied.

"What are we going to do with the computer dork?" Fox asked eagerly. "I doubt he will put up much of a fight."

"We need to find the origin of the data he sent to George Temple and why he did it. If he won't give us what we want, we will take him into custody. Though his record says to kill him on site and destroy everything he owns, something tells me he will be able to read the data card."

Fox sat back and crossed her arms, then said, "He better have some friends that attack you so I have something to do."

Tommy said, "Come on now, you make a great look-out."

"You know I can do plenty more than that Tommy," Fox pouted, "You make a great side of beef, you lug head!"

Tommy laughed, "I was just messin' with ya. I know you're scary as shit Fox...from a distance. Up close–" he stood up and placed his huge hand on the top of her head and said "you're just a small fry."

"Whatever," Fox said as she tossed a piece of gum in her mouth and chewed it repeatedly. She slapped his hand away. He threw them up feigning surrender then sat down again.

As the ship flew north, the rain turned to snow and became increasingly heavy. They reached the hills surrounding the target. Fox hopped onto a nearby mountain top overlooking the cabin below. They watched on the map as Fox highlighted the building, and the single heat signature in the west side of the main room.

"No additional hostiles," Fox said with obvious boredom in her voice over the radio channel. "He's all alone."

"Let's drop right outside the front door and enter fast," The End said, marking the drop point on the map.

"Can't wait," Tommy said while holding his Thompson sub-machine gun in both hands and stretching his shoulders.

The cold hit her immediately as she stood in two feet of sludgy brown snow with Tommy looming behind her. Snow flurried around them and the small house was about thirty feet ahead. The End sprinted towards it, activating Ker and hold-ing it parallel to the ground on her right side as she pushed through the deep snow. When she reached the door, she slashed diagonally upward at it, and then spun to the side as Tommy charged straight through the door. She stepped into the doorway as Tommy flew through the door and crashed into her, sending both of them rolling through the snow.

"Multiple unidentified contacts!" the electronic voice said from within the house.

"What the fuck hit you guys?" Fox yelled.

Tommy was crawling to his feet and replied, "It's a goddamn robot."

"I can't see it on thermal!" Fox said. "Changing up my scopes hang tight!"

The robot stepped outside of the house. It was eight feet tall at the shoulder: a mass of matte gray metal with hulking long arms that it walked in conjunction with shorter back legs like a gorilla. Its head was a convexed cylinder with a lit up red strip where its eyes would be, intersected by a vertical strip that formed a T shape.

"I'm just getting warmed up!" the electronic voice said as it rotated its head toward the mountaintop where Fox was. Suddenly a rocket screamed out of its shoulder mounted launcher and curved towards the mountain.

"Fox, incoming missile! Get out!" The End shouted over the comm channel.

The mountaintop exploded a few seconds later, enveloped in a massive fireball which bathed the entire valley in a momentary orange light. The force of the explosion shook the ground and knocked the accumulated snow off the roof. Then the high-pitched repetitive whine of the modified Thompson gun filled the winter air as Tommy engaged the robot. It spun its eye back toward him as a few rounds peppered its broad chest. It activated a blue oval-shaped energy shield along its long left forearm and held it up to block the plasma rounds. The rounds sprayed in all directions, bouncing off the shield's surface like BBs on metal.

The End did a roll maneuver to position herself behind the robot while it focused on Tommy. It noticed her and spun its head fully around to face her. She reared back with Ker and swung forward for an attack, but the robot unleashed a lightning-fast rear kick, hitting her square in the chest. She dropped Ker mid-air and landed about thirty feet away, buried in the snow.

Dazed and gasping for air, she looked to see the ape-like robot galloping towards Tommy. It slammed into his gun with its shield arm, disarming him and tossing it aside. With its other arm it grabbed Tommy by the neck and lifted his 280 pound frame off the ground without straining in the slightest.

Tommy looked straight into the robot's glowing red eye stripe and said, "Fuck you robot. If you're gonna kill me, hurry it up."

The metal head shifted back and forth rapidly for a moment as if it was struggling to react, then a blinding white line cut through its head from the left side. The flash of light diminished and everything fell back into darkness. Glowing molten metal dripped from the entry and exit holes in the robot's head, and the light in its eye went dark.

"I got the bastard," Fox said between heavy breaths over the comms.

Tommy responded through a clenched jaw, "Yeah, you got him, but it's still choking me out! Do something!"

Another silent white line flashed for a moment, hitting the robot in the wrist and severing its hand. Tommy fell to the ground and pried the massive cold hand off of his throat. He threw it into the field and yelled out in relief. He kneeled in the snow and coughed, trying to catch his breath.

"Nice shooting, Fox," The End said while walking towards the pulverized door of the house, clutching her side with one arm and leaning down to retrieve Ker with the other. "Are you okay?"

Fox replied, "Yeah. I think so. I'm half buried though. Gunther, can you pull me up?"

The recon ship circled around to the top of the mountain and transported her into the ship. It was veiled by the snowstorm, but its faint engines could be heard reverberating off the hills surrounding the valley.

"I gotcha," Gunther said. "Still showing one heat sig in the house."

"That motherfucker. Where are you?" The End said while storming into the doorway. Tommy found his mangled Thompson gun, picked it up off the ground, and followed her in.

The inside of the house was warm. It had an old-fashioned wood burning stove in the corner and was eerily dark. All of the windows were covered in tacky maroon curtains. A small kitchen was off to the left, with dirty linoleum tile floors and dishes covering the counters and sink. The living room was also dark, save for the lights from the multitude of screens.

A man sat on the couch facing a wall-mounted flat screen television. The image on the TV displayed a video game: a first-person perspective of the player holding a rifle, standing in a forest, with the green landscape and bodies of water arching upwards on the horizon into an enormous loop. Along the wall perpendicular to the TV was a myriad of computers, monitors, and servers. He had enough tech to fill a command center.

He slowly turned towards them and The End noticed his hands were shaking. He was a bald, lanky man, and likely in his sixties. He was dressed in pajama pants, a ratty old t-shirt and a dark hoodie. He had grown an unkempt gray beard and wore thin rectangular-framed glasses. He held up his hands in fear as he spoke.

"Did you guys kill Burrus? I swear I never would have made him attack you, he was for the typical UO plebs, not for The End for Christ's sake."

"You have an illegal robot that you designed to kill United Order agents, and you didn't mean for it to attack me?" The End said angrily, then walked over to him and grabbed his shirt, pulling him to his feet. "That thing almost killed my friends!"

The man's eyes bulged as he tapped on The End's chest plate. "He almost killed you too," he said hoarsely.

The End dropped him onto the couch and looked down. She had a huge dent in her chest plate below her breasts, caved in a few inches where the robot had kicked her. She felt thankful for her armor for the first time since she became an executioner.

The man continued, "I changed his programming so he would be a better friend to me, just some custom dialogue options and new learning algorithms, but I didn't build him. I don't design machines of war. I stole him from a UO facility. Freed him, really."

Her heart was still pounding from the adrenaline coursing through her system. She looked back at the man and said, "Well, it's dead and you're next, understand?"

The man's face changed to despair as he said "No, please! I'm not doing anything here okay? I never hurt anyone."

"That's what every single piece of scum says to me right before they die. You call yourself Arbiter, right? Why?" The End asked.

Fox interrupted over the comms channel, "It means a great influencer of cultural change. Sounds a bit arrogant to me."

Arbiter heard her and said, "Lady on the radio is well-educated. Don't overthink it, it's from a video game."

"Shut the fuck up, incel," The End said and raised her fist to threaten him. "Tell me your relationship to George Temple or I'm gonna break some teeth."

"He was...my friend." His eyes welled with tears as he said, "I was playing games with George over the last year on our hidden private network. It's how I met him. UO monitors all official servers. It was the only way we could talk freely...like the old days."

"Do you spread conspiracy theories to everyone you game with?" The End asked.

"We often talked about how corrupt the administration is. How none of it made sense. Then, Michael Grad broke into a UO complex and stole proof of their corruption. He posted it on Verge, an underground social media site of sorts."

"I know what it is," The End said. "We've purged it many times but it just keeps coming back, like cancer."

"There are so few of us now. I'm not sure if anyone else even saw Grad's data before it was taken down, but I had enough time to make a copy of it. After I learned the truth, I couldn't stop drinking. I knew the sins that humanity had committed, and that it was too late to fix it. Misery loves company, as they say, so one night I was drunk and told George everything. It changed him, as it would change anyone to know the truth about what happened. He had to see for himself. He didn't care about anything else but seeing that proof. So, I sent it to him."

The man buried his head in his hands, muffling his voice as he continued, "And then you killed him, along with Michael."

"Michael Grad was a terrorist. Just another wacko that shot up his workplace," Tommy said.

"That was the story the media told. Clearly, you just believe everything they feed you," Arbiter said while scowling at Tommy. "I'm sure you believe the soot in the water supply is safe to drink too."

Tommy popped his knuckles and replied, "Look, I don't do too well with disrespect."

"Why don't you go ask General McMillan about the shooting?" Arbiter continued. "He knows that was an attack on a government facility...an archive for everything this government wants hidden."

The End decided to steer the conversation away from her father. "Your buddy George was threatening the security of the United Order of America. He had the data that you sent him. I have it right here," The End said while holding up the data card.

"The fact that they had you kill George just for possessing it kind of shows that it's true, doesn't it?" he said and smirked.

The End scoffed and said, "UO flatcaps charged him with possessing gold dust. Did you know he was a duster?"

Arbiter laughed and said, "Absolute rubbish. It was because of the data."

"I'll decide that myself. I know you have a secure way of reading it."

"Give me the card," he said as he took it from her hands and sat at his computer station. His chair squeaked as he swiveled to face the computer, and he began talking quickly.

"I can read it, but the data is scanned in a way that any time it is read the location is pinged. Luckily, this house is a complete dead zone for long-range signals," he said as he furiously typed on his keyboard. "It's blocking any signals to and from your citizen devices too. Don't worry, you can speak freely. No one can listen to us here." He motioned over to the largest monitor in his setup. The display flashed in and showed what looked like security footage.

He sped up the footage which showed a crew of three young men building a metal frame base with a quadrupedal leg structure extending from the base to the floor. Then, a torso was added on top of the base, and then arms, and finally the head. It looked like a metal centaur skeleton, with movable joints along the legs, arms, and spinal column.

"Here you go," Arbiter said. "The famed Enlightened One. I remember when this monstrosity landed. I thought humanity was going to be saved too. A higher intelligence was going to show us how to be better. Eliminate avarice, hunger, inequity, disease, violence...share their tech with us."

They were mesmerized by the footage which showed the metal frame being powered by batteries and motors, eventually having the ability to be controlled remotely. It could seamlessly walk, open doors, jump, and carry boxes. At one point the robot was surrounded by its designers as they simultaneously kicked it again and again to check its balance and recovery. It was remarkably good at staying on its feet and adapting to inclines. They poured soapy water on a ramp to make it able to adapt to slick surfaces.

Arbiter continued, "But, that isn't what happened. The encounter was faked and the scheme played on people's emotions to garner a massive following. The war to occupy every continent had begun. Their goal was to reshape the world into a single religion, to oppress all others, and to take away citizen's freedoms so they were easier to control. It was the ultimate justification to kill anyone that opposed them."

The video showed the men adding on elastic layers over the robotic frame, then green rubber parts designed to look like muscles. They painted the outside skin layer, adding fine details to the robot's face, installing lifelike eyes that tracked movement realistically, and added details to the jaw to make it believable when it spoke. It transformed from its metal framework into the alien seen in the infamous news casts: the Enlightened One, undoubtedly. The video continued with them testing speech patterns and accents as the robot recited the same speech he would give to the President. It cut to a conversation between a team of programmers about introducing a new type of AI for military use in other robots when Arbiter stopped the video.

The End felt light-headed and put one hand onto the wall to keep her balance. She felt something change inside her. The pride for her nation and the work she had done was no more. In its place was a burning hatred for the corrupt leaders that used her as a puppet, and all of the soldiers they used to conquer and spread their lies around the world. Then an immense sadness overtook the anger as she thought about all of the people who were no longer free to live their lives, and for the billions who had their lives taken from them in the name of this false war. She felt the weight of all of the people her squad had killed on the battlefield pushing down on her.

With her bottom lip shaking she said, "I can't believe this." She took several deep breaths to calm herself down, and suppressed the rage of emotions she was feeling, but couldn't stop a few tears from coming.

"That's some freaky shit," Tommy said. "Was the thing that almost killed me built by these guys too?"

"Burrus had been with me for years. I found out that they were making another variant of robot...ones for use in battle. The project was canceled since the curtains were closing on the war. So, I hijacked one of them. The apes were controlled remotely, allowing me to take it over after hacking into one of the units. Burrus woke up from the storage location and was fully in my control. After I used him to destroy the other ape-like robots, I made him smash his way out through the concrete walls that were holding him, and took out some guards that were in the way."

The End laughed and wiped her face with her fingers. She said, "That's a bold move. Can't say I wouldn't want one of them on my side."

Arbiter laughed nervously and said, "I reprogrammed him so he identified me as friendly and anyone associated with UO was an enemy. He was a beast. I mean, he flew off the wall when you guys broke in here; I've never seen him go that hard before. He was seriously throwing down."

"He ruined my Thompson," Tommy said and held up his mangled machine gun. "I thought I was toast, but Fox brought down the holy light on him."

Arbiter looked down and said, "So that would be Commander Jenning that killed Burrus. LT-52 Light Rifle. Her flashlight is about the only thing that could breach his armor."

"Why is he talking about me?" Fox said over comms.

He furrowed his brow, smiled slyly and said, "That's right. I know all about you, and I know about you, Jack Thompson. I even know about your mysterious pilot. However," he spun towards The End and motioned toward her with his hands flatly pressed together, "You were the enigma. They don't keep any data on you out in the open. I had to dig for it, seemingly endlessly."

The End stepped back and felt her cheeks turn red.

Tommy cleared his throat, "You only know us through what you saw on a computer. That means you don't know us at all."

"I'm familiar with your military careers. I know what you all have sacrificed in the name of these lies. But you all can still do the right thing."

The End stepped forward and clenched her fists, "They are going to pay for this. They are all going to pay."

"I don't think their debts to humanity can ever be repaid," Arbiter said while running his fingers through his beard. "Look, what are we doing here anyways? You guys have seen the damn vids – I'd like to get on with fixing Burrus to be honest."

The End stared him in the eyes and said, "Is it going to attack us again?"

"No, no, no. Not to worry, I'll give him a quick update and he'll be right as rain."

"Listen," she said, "we could use you. You could help us put an end to all of this and stop the United Order."

Arbiter sighed and his face paled. He took a deep breath and said, "Yeah I'm in. But, only if Burrus can join us."

"You can fix him? How long is that going to take?" Tommy asked.

"One day. We are gonna need him, trust me," Arbiter said and stood up. He extended his right hand towards The End and said, "Shake on it." The End shook his hand, then he pulled it away and tried to hide the pain of her grip.

"Done. We also need to come up with a plan to distribute these videos, and any other data you have against the administration." The End said.

"E, are you sure about this?" Tommy said. "Talk about kicking a hornet's nest."

"That would be extremely difficult," Arbiter said. "United Order has the best security in the world. Everyone is always looking for vulnerabilities, but few find any. When poking around in restricted systems is punishable by death, hackers tend to change professions because, well, you've killed them." He paused, stroking his beard with his left hand in thought. "However, you should have top level clearance, E. Can I call you E? It's just generally better I think. It feels weird calling you The End."

"I can use my clearance to get into the United Order Library. I can add the files to the archive and they would be accessible by anyone with a citizen device." The End said, ignoring his question.

Arbiter cleared his throat. "That would work. However, the United Order would ultimately control the files. They would simply erase the data from the Library once they found out what you had done. Then they wouldn't be available to anyone any longer."

The End tapped her chin in thought. "Well, what would you need my clearance for then?"

Arbiter walked over to his desk and put his hands on it, "I could see a way that we could upload the evidence as raw files, use your access to broadcast the data to everyone's citizen device via the UO Emergency Broadcasting service and everyone can simply peruse them as they please, and save them, and copy them."

"They couldn't do a damn thing about it after that." The End said.

He nodded. "The raw files would actually exist on the individual devices. So the only way to get them back would be to physically take them back, which hopefully will be impossible due to a citizen uprising."

Tommy slapped his hands together and said, "Just like that, huh? Just like that? You think it's going to be that easy?"

Arbiter glanced around at them quickly, "Or...we get caught and executed in front of millions of people." He held his hand outstretched towards them and said, "Or, even worse, the people just won't care. They'll downplay it, play it safe, and stay oppressed. I fear we may have come too far to reverse the damage."

The End put her hand on top of Arbiter's. Tommy shook his head and said, "You all are out of your minds...but I'm in." He put his hand on top of The End's, then together they all lowered them.

"What about Fox and Gunther?" Tommy said. They need to see what the Enlightened One really is."

Fox's voice came over the comms and said, "I would like to see that. It sounds...interesting."

The End and Tommy walked out of the cabin and into the snowstorm. Arbiter followed them out and was holding a spare head for his robot.

"I'll set up the broadcasting equipment. Meet me here in a day or so. I'll be in touch," he said as he stopped at the frozen metal figure. "Thanks for not killing me."

She stopped and smiled at him. Then they were transported back to the ship hovering overhead.

Arbiter gripped the robot's damaged head and spun it counter-clockwise. Eventually it popped off and he tossed it to the ground. He placed the new head into the opening and screwed it down until it clicked into place. He tapped a few commands in the device to boot the robot's root operating system so it could only be controlled remotely. The T-shaped screen on its head lit up in a bright green color, then faded into an image of a gorilla's face with closed eyes.

"Come on, man, it's cold out here." Arbiter pleaded.

Suddenly, the eyes opened and Burrus' yellow eyes looked back at Arbiter.

"Yes!" Arbiter yelled.

The robot held up its severed wrist and inspected it.

"I know, big fella. Let's go inside and get you all fixed up," the man said as they turned together and walked through the dark sludge towards the cabin. "I've got a few software updates for you too. We made some friends!"

A hundred yards overhead, Fox sat on the bench in the hold of the ship, holding her hand over her mouth with her other hand shakily holding the hacked citizen device as she watched. As she watched more footage, they discovered even more evidence against the United Order. Footage of the saucer flying around the desert. Test flights with human pilots. Engineers explaining how the gyro engine kept it in the air. Interviews, tax receipts, journals, orders. One piece of evidence that Fox lazily walked over to The End and shoved in her face was an order to have the Articles of Ascension created, signed by a man named Frances McMillan. The orders were signed before he was a general.

It showed that before the Enlightened One landed, the then-President's cabinet had decided to create the Articles of Ascension to embody their own fantasy world. These indisputable laws, penned by what people thought was a being that could easily annihilate us if we chose to disobey them, were really designed by old white people. One of them was her father.

The End slid down the hull of the ship, clutching her head with both hands, and crouching in the fetal position. Tears fell through the gaps in the metal grate below her, down into the belly of the ship as it swayed slightly back and forth, forging a path through the snowstorm. She wondered which article he came up with. Was it that 'The Sole Religion is Christianity: Its guiding principles will keep the darkness at bay'?

Was it the sexuality ban? Was it the outlaw of computers that were not monitored and provided by the United Order? Was it that any country who drew arms against us would be exiled completely from the rapidly expanding United Order of America, and declared an enemy of the planet? That drug use was a supreme offense? Was it all of them? She felt like she was going to throw up.

Fox was pacing around in a panic and said, "Are we really gonna do this? Are we really going up against people capable of doing these things? They won't let this information leak. They'll do anything to keep it buried. We'll be killed."

The End let go of her head and looked up at Fox, who had stopped pacing and returned her stare. "Maybe we will have the chance to die for something that matters. Most people just die from cancer."

"I guess so," Fox said dismally.

"We can't let them get away with this," Tommy said. "We all know what this led to. The nuke trades that lasted for months. You remember Toronto, on the outskirts after it got hit. You know exactly what I'm talking about."

"I remember," The End said. "All of those people just trying to get out of the city and away from the radiation. UO gunned them all down. They deserve justice. The whole planet does."

Fox nodded. "Okay. Okay I'm in."

The End spoke loudly, "Gunther, are you in?"

The pilot gave a thumbs up.

"Good," The End said as she grinned. "Take me home. I've got work in the morning. I'm just going to keep normal for the next thirteen hours. You guys need to stay in contact with Arbiter and check his progress. Hopefully he can follow through with his idea to get the word out."

Tommy and Fox nodded.

After a long flight back, The End was transported straight into her bedroom once again. She struggled to unbuckle her heavy shoulder pauldrons, but once they were on the floor with her vambraces she could move a little more easily. The dented breastplate was a bear to get loose, but she finally was able to unclasp the releases under her armpits and set the hefty piece of metal on the floor. Then she carefully bent down and removed her greaves and boots, so she was able to freely move in her body-suit base layer.

She removed the base layer and inspected herself in the tall mirror propped up in the corner of her room. There was a large, dark bruise covering the area below her sternum and the top half of her stomach that reached around her right side. She was completely exhausted but couldn't get into her bed without washing the brown slime off of her skin. She sat on the floor of the shower as the hot water washed the storm off of her. She scrubbed herself furiously with a pumice stone to get the oily filth off, a lengthy task that she had become accustomed to. Her bottom ribs hurt immensely when she put pressure on them, but didn't feel broken.

Afterwards, she shuffled over to her night stand and grabbed a bottle of painkillers, then took some with a glass of water. She crawled into the bed and carefully pulled the covers over her body. She rested in the fetal position, clutching her ribs with one arm, and promptly fell asleep.

She managed to get five hours of semi-uninterrupted sleep before her citizen device woke her for work. She turned off the alarm, sat up in her bed, and stuck out her chest to pop her back and sternum. There was pain but it was manageable. She took a few more painkillers and went into the bathroom to get ready.

On the Justice Floor, her makeup crew gathered around her to try to fix her lazy work. She just didn't care any longer.

"Hey," a suit said to her. "What's wrong? You don't look like yourself today."

She smiled at her and bucked up a little to try to act normal. The last thing she wanted to do was raise suspicion. "Sorry, just partied a little too hard last night."

"I don't blame you. The last show was amazing, highest viewership in a while. You killed it!"

Her introduction was not as lengthy as last time. There wasn't anyone as high profile as Michael Grad on the block so the viewership was sure to be lower. She waved at the crowd and stood next to her three new patients, squirming beneath their hoods like they always did. They seemed a little more vocal than usual, but their gags were still keeping them quiet.

The announcer started, "Our first criminal chose to live her life as a devout Muslim, which is a direct affront to the one true Christian God of the United Order. We all know that in order to survive as a species we must do all that we can to quell these insignificant religions with their sick doctrines. We'd send her back to the Middle East and let her scavenge the radioactive wastes with the rest of her people, but we might as well let The End take a swing! The End is here to do just that. Whenever you are ready, my dear."

The End walked up to the first chair and yanked back the hood. Beneath it was a black woman with some gray showing in her long, gorgeous, curly hair, and the same green, pleading eyes she had seen in the park. It was Gracie, bound to the chair, muzzled, and staring desperately at The End as tears streamed down her cheeks. The End completely froze for several seconds as her heart beat relentlessly.

"Hey!" a raspy voice called out from the balcony seat overlooking the stage. The End turned toward the voice. The Anointed One was standing with his hands on the railing and leaning towards her. "Kill her, that's your job isn't it?" he said before erupting in a coughing frenzy. He struggled to speak, but said "Don't you want her to kill the Muslim, everyone?"

The crowd cheered, and The End clenched her jaw in anger as she stared at the Anointed One. She took Ker out of the holster and activated it while staring into his eyes.

She turned towards Gracie, mouthed "I'm so sorry" to her, reared Ker back and swung it sideways across all three of the patient's shoulders, beheading them all with a single swing. The speed and wide arc of the attack splattered blood across the chest of the host's tuxedo and out into the audience, spattering some onto the Anointed One's sagging face as well. The patient's heads rolled to the ground, and the crowd cheered wildly. The End turned and stared at the Anointed One, who looked shocked as he frantically tried to wipe the blood with a napkin. Then she holstered Ker and stormed off stage.

In the elevator, she said "Heaven's Reach" and rode up to the roof. She walked through the chilly rain and grabbed the railing, then screamed at the top of her lungs across the ominous cityscape. When she ran out of breath, she collapsed onto the wet gravel spread across the rooftop and wept. The horses stirred and watched her with their glowing eyes, pulling gently against their chains.

She hated herself for killing Gracie. She weighed all the outcomes in her head and realized there was nothing else she could've done. If she would've attacked the Anointed One, his flatcaps might have stopped her. Even if she somehow succeeded, she would be captured and her plan would be foiled. She did what she had to do. She kept repeating that to herself as she rocked back and forth with her head in her hands.

Her citizen device started ringing and she almost threw it off the ledge, but she realized it was coming from the new one that Arbiter had given her. She tapped the screen and answered the call.

"Hello?" Arbiter said. "I saw what happened. You were in a tough spot, E."

"I shouldn't have killed her, man. She didn't do anything wrong," The End said between sniffles. "He made me do it…that bastard. Just like he has made me do everything else in my life. I can't do this anymore. I can't."

"I know, E. I'm so sorry. We will get him back for it, don't worry."

She climbed to her feet and walked over to the yellow-eyed horse named War. "We need to. There is no other option." She touched its metallic neck, running her fingers across the small cracks between each section of its interlocked sections. War stared back at her without expression.

"I ran into a complication with the broadcast," Arbiter continued. "The security preventing remote broadcast is completely impenetrable. The only place that we'll be able to send a signal is within the Capitol Building itself, on the Justice Floor. I'm working on compressing the data so that it can be distributed more quickly."

"Good idea. We can do it during tomorrow's show. I can broadcast it myself and—" her original citizen device started ringing, and she saw it was her father calling. "I gotta run and deal with some fallout from today I think. I'll call you later," she said and disconnected.

She hesitantly answered the call from General McMillan, "Hey Dad."

"I saw that display you put on today. I have to be honest...it doesn't look good. I've tried to convince the Anointed One that you are just being overly emotional, but it hasn't been easy."

"I know. I'm sorry about the way I acted. Maybe doing this job for so long has started to wear me down a little bit."

"Don't you remember what I taught you? About Mastro Titta?"

"I remember everything you taught me, father," she said as Death, the horse with purple eyes, pranced across the rooftop, stopping just as it reached the limit of its chain.

"He executed people for the Pope for sixty eight years. Sixty. Eight. That's what I had planned for you. A legacy like that to be proud of. Administering the will of the divine."

"I know, father. I promise I can do better."

"Why don't you come to the Library so we can discuss this? I think we can still salvage your position. We'll go over the details."

"Okay Dad, see you soon," she said and ended the call. She stroked War's long face for a moment and looked across the vast cityscape below. In the distance, a slow, shimmering wave enveloped the dark skyscrapers.

"Have you ever seen the sun?" she asked the horse. It stared back at her with still yellow eyes.

"Of course not," she said. "You're trapped here too." It didn't react.

"You really are just a travesty, aren't you? Not like a real horse at all, just a tool for them to use." She put her elbows on the railing and held her head in her hands and looked over the edge. "Perhaps we aren't so different." Her cloak billowed in the wind as the storm worsened.

Over the vast cityscape, an enormous lightning bolt flashed onto the lightning rod on an adjacent skyscraper. The chemicals in the air around it ignited from the heat, flaring along the bolt's path like a finger made of fire reaching down from the heavens. The firebolt quickly dissipated into black smoke along with the menacing crack of thunder and the rushing sound of the billowing inferno that followed.

She climbed onto the wide cement barrier and stood with the city at her feet. More firebolts branched into the vast city, and the blue and orange light from each strike simultaneously scattered through the raindrops, creating a full color spectrum reflection that cascaded across the sky. She loved watching the shimmers during firestorms, moving like vertical waves across the sky in brief, and beautiful rainbows. She always imagined they made her more powerful, as if the air around her could suddenly burst into flames at any moment.

She walked into the elevator and said "Library". The elevator took her down to the floor given to her father by the administration. She stepped into the antechamber decorated with gray granite walls, with sections of downward-flowing water spaced evenly along them. Behind the water was screen paneling that could display any color. Her father chose an ominous red glow. She hated how erratic and evil it looked.

She continued down a corridor into the library. This room did not have the flowing water effect on the walls, and the wall screens were displaying text from all of the articles in the library. These servers held all of the authorized knowledge of the world. McMillan and his team had been collecting, editing, and rewriting the history of the world for the past twenty years and beyond, storing it on the drives in the library. Any data that was stored privately outside the library was confiscated, reviewed, and stored if it was deemed necessary knowledge humans would need to keep moving forward.

Those were the words of the administration, anyways. Once added to the library, it could be accessed by any citizen device. She saw her father standing behind a desk at the far end of the room looking down at a computer screen. The blue light of the screen made him look paler than usual.

"Hello daughter," he said in a stern voice. "I never got an update on the hacker. What happened in Nova Scotia?"

"He wasn't there. Like you said, he knew we were coming. We torched the place though."

"I see. Why did you hesitate when killing your prisoner today?"

"Because... I knew she wasn't a Muslim. I hesitated because I thought there may have been a mistake. We wouldn't intentionally mislabel someone for execution, would we?"

He smiled and said, "Only when we need to. She knew things that she shouldn't have. Believed things she shouldn't believe. She didn't get any of those ideas in your head, did she?"

"I already told you, she told me some typical conspiracy theory crap. I've heard it before and didn't consider it valid. You're not saying there was any truth in what she said, are you?"

"No. I'm saying she was spreading lies about the administration," General McMillan said. "We simply construed to the public that she was being executed for something else. That way it doesn't make people wonder just what specific information she was spreading. It's a strategy we've deployed to keep a lid on these bogus theories that people tend to cling to."

"I understand, father."

"I'm still concerned about the way you hesitated. It shouldn't matter to you what people are up there for. You're not the judge, you're the executioner. You should just swing your ax, that's it."

"I understand, father."

"Well I'm afraid that isn't good enough. The Anointed One has decided that you are to be replaced as head executioner until you can make amends."

She stood at attention and said with a firm voice, "I've killed thousands for the cause of this administration. My loyalty was never in question."

"It wasn't until recently. But we have found some things that are troubling."

"What do you mean?"

He crossed his arms and there was anger in his voice, "I know what you have been up to, kid. My job is information. The only way to stay in control is to monitor everything and everyone, including the head executioner. I know you've been talking to the hacker. You let him live, disobeying the death order that we placed upon him. I've dispatched my own team to take care of him."

"I was keeping him alive because he might have more information that would've helped us—"

"Enough!" the General said and slammed both fists onto the table. "I know you're lying."

"You've been lying to me my whole life, father," The End said, her expression changing to anger. "You said Michael Grad was just another crazy citizen. Not a revolutionary that successfully stole proof of the sins of this administration!"

"You think humanity could handle the truth? It would plunge the world into chaos yet again. I will not let you destroy what we have built, even if you are my daughter."

The End watched as a figure entered the room, cloaked in darkness. It was a man, dressed in a hooded cowl that was similar to her own. His armor was black and shiny, and consisted of large spiked shoulder pauldrons, sleek vambraces, greaves, boots, and epaulets. Across his eyes was a black visor with dark red eyes that were faintly illuminated. Everything about him was darkness and death. She noticed faint trails of smoke coming out of the eyes, slowly floating upwards and out of the top of the hood.

"Who the fuck are you?" she said to the man.

"Why, that's your replacement," the General said. "The Cleanser."

"You didn't recognize my armor," The Cleanser said. "It's the same one from the movie, but this one isn't a prop; it's battle ready." He began slowly walking across the room, placing himself between her and the General. "Thanks for giving me this opportunity, traitor. Come quietly so you don't get hurt."

"Kevin. There is no way you will be able to handle this job. You're just an actor. I am justice, not you. So—" she unsheathed Ker and it cackled as the pink light formed across the sharp edge of the ax, "kindly get the fuck out of my way."

The Cleanser pulled his cloak to the side, revealing the long blade at his hip. The sword was over five feet long, the tip touched the ground and the hilt reached up to his collarbone. He unclasped the release on the sheath and pulled the blade out, then held it up in front of him.

"They built this claymore especially for me. I call it Moros," he said as he activated it. It had black plasma coils along the length of the blade on both sides. When it hissed to life, the unnatural glow of black light encased the blade.

"Do you even know how to use that thing?" The End asked.

"I do, actually. Don't you remember me in Seaman's Galley? I learned swordplay for my role. I had my own trainer and everything."

"That movie was utter shit."

"You know, I actually liked you, E. It's nothing personal, you know that, right? I gotta do what's best for me, and in this case, what's best for the world."

"You don't have the slightest clue what you're doing," she said while taking a step toward him.

"It's easy. All I have to do is touch you with this blade anywhere on that little body of yours and you will die," The Cleanser said as he began walking toward her. "Painfully."

"Good luck," The End said, then sprinted directly towards him while swinging her ax above her head. He didn't expect her bold aggression and drew back defensively. Just before she was within swinging range, she dropped into a low slide along the floor. As she slid, The Cleanser raised Moros over his head and attacked using a downward thrust. The End barely made it past the blade, it pierced her cape as she slid beneath it, and the hefty claymore dug deep into the floor. The inertia sliced her cape cleanly in half down the middle and she came out of her slide into a crouched position beneath him.

As he struggled to pull the blade out from the floor, The End spun from underneath him, swinging Ker in a wide arc to build maximum momentum, then slammed the ax head against the blade of the sword. The force from the blow sent Kevin against the wall across from her and into all of the monitors that were fastened to it, sending arcs of electricity across his entire body.

She stood and sheathed her ax. Moros was still impaled into the ground next to her. She grabbed the long hilt and pulled it from the stone, turned toward her father and pointed its menacing blade straight at his head. She stormed toward the bewildered General and said, "Nice try replacing me with an actor. That worked out well."

"Backup!" he called out. The End grabbed him by the uniform and slammed him against the monitor behind him. The screen flickered and flashed, with lines of broken pixels splintering from the impact point. "You wouldn't kill your own father, would you?" he asked with fear in his eyes.

"You wouldn't help elevate a politician to the status of a god, knowing that it wasn't true, resulting in the elimination of billions of people, would you?" she asked.

The General stared at her, searching her face for some semblance of mercy.

Then, multiple flatcap units stormed in from every doorway, armed with non-lethal taserswarm launchers. They opened fire with a volley of barbs, blasting out of the round, silver, barrels of their weapons in clusters. They were short, stubby, rifles that fired in bursts and hissed loudly each time the chamber depressurized. Hundreds of the piercing needles hit her armor and deflected off harmlessly. The volleys continued relentlessly as she sprang into action.

She grabbed her cape in one hand and spun rapidly around, deflecting a batch of needles with the fabric, then swung Moros defensively, slashing groups of the projectiles out of the air. She quickly whipped the claymore through the air and released it, sending it end over end across the room before impaling a flatcap's head to the wall.

She summoned Ker from its holster and swung it around in a defensive whirlwind, causing a few of the taser wires to wrap around the staff of the ax. She aggressively yanked them forward, sending two flatcaps flailing through the air towards her as they refused to let go of their weapons. They crashed to the floor in front of her and scrambled to stand up. She reared back and cut through both of their armored heads in a single swing as they screamed for mercy.

More shots bounced off of her armor before she felt one of the barbs go through her hood and embed into her skin just above her right ear. The electricity flowed down the wire and throughout her entire body until she couldn't stand any longer. She fell to the ground and watched Ker slip from her fingers and deactivate.

Shiny black boots stopped in front of the golden ax handle. She was straining to reach it as the black gauntlet reached down and picked it up.

"She is disarmed," The Cleanser said while putting the hilt of Ker on his belt. The electric pulses stopped and The End could move again. She grabbed the barb with her hand and ripped it out of her skin, crying out in pain. She began to stand when The Cleanser unleashed a kick to her stomach where she was previously injured from Burrus. She felt it dent in her armor as she slid across the floor and crashed against the wall. She doubled over from the excruciating pain and the wind getting knocked out of her. She laid still, groaning and trying to catch her breath.

"Look at her gasp," the voice said. The surviving flatcaps who gathered around her laughed.

General McMillan walked closer to her. "It is unimaginable what you were planning to do. You have completely disgraced me and you are no longer my daughter." He turned toward The Cleanser and said, "We must deal with this quickly. You will bring her to justice tomorrow. Let's see how ready you are to take this role." He turned and walked out of the room without looking back.

The Cleanser crouched down next to her again and lifted his visor. Beneath it were the light blue eyes she recognized, the face at one point she thought was handsome and charming. Now he just looked pathetic, like a little boy dressing up as a super villain.

He lowered his voice and said, "That's what you get for trying to betray us, traitor. And you know what fate awaits traitors better than anyone. I'm going to take your corpse up to Heaven's Reach and make those machines quarter you. That will be a show to remember."

The End struggled to find breath but was able to say, "Fuck...you...asshole."

The Cleanser rose to his feet and kicked her again in the stomach. This time it opened a wound, and she felt the warm blood dripping down the inside of her armor.

He grabbed her by the chin, the sharp edges of his gloved hand cutting into her, and said, "I can't wait until tomorrow. I will forever be known as the executioner who executed The End." He wiped the corner of his mouth with his other armored hand. "I was looking forward to killing your old team as well," he said and flipped his visor down, covering his eyes again. "They were traitors too after all."

Smoke poured out of his fake, glowing, red eyes on his visor. He slowly pulled his hood over his head and said, "We weren't sure what you were gonna do. After your pilot told us that they were conspirators, we put them up there as a tactic to force you to quit. But you didn't even take their hoods off before killing them. You really were the best at what you did, executing three at once...but I'll be better." The Cleanser stood up and ordered, "Take this bitch to her cell."

Though the breath had been kicked from her, his words felt like a knife in her gut. The End panicked, couldn't breathe and wasn't sure she cared enough to. She would never forgive herself for what she had done. Fox and Tommy were dead by her hand. Her closest friends turned from being her companions to being her victims, bitten by Ker for doing nothing but helping her. If only she had pulled their hoods back to see their faces, she would have saved them.

The flatcaps dragged her through the room, her metal boots brushing the corpses of the men that she had killed, her tattered cape dragging through their blood and streaking it across the white floor. Her spirit was broken. She couldn't move and didn't want to. She felt like never moving again and felt there was no reason to. She couldn't wait until the next day. She would sit in her chair and be swiftly killed, just as all of her victims had been. She would finally be rid of the incessant pain of this pointless, treacherous world. She would be free from it at last.

She laid on the cold floor in the white-walled cell they threw her in. In the hours she sat under the fluorescent lights, she had accepted her death. For the things she had done throughout her life, she had to be punished, and was fully ready to accept her sentence. There was a glimpse of hope that she could change the world for the better and right the wrongs of those who were in charge and abused their power, but that hope had dissipated into the empty darkness within her. There was no changing it at this point.

Those corrupt individuals would remain in power and, who knows, perhaps the world was better off in the long run that way. Maybe the damage was already done, and humanity could somehow bounce back from the destruction, disease, and addiction that plagued it. She just wished the leaders of the United Order would also be killed for the evil they wrought on the world.

I almost killed them, she thought as she rolled onto her side, clutching her bruised stomach. She ran her hand across the dent The Cleanser had made in her armor and wondered if Arbiter was still alive. She could only hear her pounding heartbeat as she felt the hatred fester within her. Her heart was pounding so hard she thought the walls of her cell were shaking.

The feeling intensified, and The End arduously pushed herself off of the floor with her palms. She could hear the tremors now – it wasn't her imagination. She walked over to her cell wall and pressed herself against it. Again she felt a quake in low, rumbling patterns. Then, right next to her head, a long metal arm crashed through the stone wall, then pulled away. She walked over and looked through the hole and saw the eyes of a gorilla staring back at her. She jumped, startled by the sight of a gorilla wearing a metal cylindrical helmet.

"Sleep well?" the robot said in a kind voice with only a hint of digitalization. The gorilla put his mechanical arm back through the hole, grasped the inside wall, and then pulled it towards him, creating a large opening. "Let's go," it said.

The End stepped through the opening and looked up at the towering robot. "Burrus, was it?" she said drearily. "Your face, it looks so real."

The yellow eyes on the screen looked responsive and lifelike as they stared back at The End. The screen was T-shaped so only the gorilla's eyes were visible, with a thin vertical strip that showed his nose and the center of his mouth. "Now would be a very good time to leave," he said with urgency.

"Lead the way," The End said. "I'm with you."

As they ran down the corridors of the prison block, a squad of flatcaps appeared in front of them and opened fire. The End stayed behind Burrus and the metal rounds rang off of his armored body, inflicting no damage at all. The hallway was filled with smoke, ricocheting shots and metal shrapnel. As Burrus ran through them, he grabbed their round cylindrical heads with his long arms and effortlessly pressed them against the wall or floor, one by one, flattening their helmets instantaneously. He exerted the exact amount of force to crush them, rolling and pivoting to keep his momentum. He was the most efficient killer The End had ever seen, even deadlier than Fox. He killed ten or so flatcaps in the quick time it took them to get to the end of the long corridor.

A flatcap walked through a doorway behind her and pressed his rifle in between her shoulder blades. "Get on the ground!" he yelled at her. Burrus turned around and saw them, but didn't calculate a feasible way to rescue her without her getting shot. She slowly lifted her arms, and, with her right arm, grabbed the barrel of the gun and pulled it forward around her right side. The flatcap fired a few fruitless rounds as she spun around. She leapt straight up and unleashed a high kick, flattening his head against the wall and crushing it into the cement. She pulled her long silver boot out of his collapsed head, shouldered his rifle, and joined Burrus at the windowed siding of the Capitol Building.

"We need to jump now," Burrus said as he slammed his fist through the immense glass window, shattering it and raining tinted glass down upon the water streets below. He grabbed The End with one arm and swung out the opening with the other, gripping onto the window edge and hanging out over the city. He released his grip and they dropped twenty floors in freefall before he forcefully shoved his hand into the concrete side of the building. He used his grip to slow down their descent and repeated this process until they reached the sidewalk safely. People on the floating walkways looked at them in awe.

"It's The End!" a little girl dressed in tattered clothing called out. Her mother glared at the executioner and the hulking robot standing beside her and shuffled the kid in the opposite direction. "She has a robot!" the little girl persisted.

They ran away from the Capitol Building down the walkways as they rose and fell with the shallow waves. They made it a few blocks and opened into a full sprint along the edge of the harbor. Suddenly, The End heard the faint flutter of engines above her. A UO recon ship was flying overhead, likely about to fire at them or attempt a capture.

"Burrus!" The End called out. The robot turned around and faced her. "Ship above! Can you take it out?"

The gorilla's eyes transitioned into a concerned expression. He replied, "There's our ride. Get aboard, and let's get out of here."

The End looked at him with a confused expression on her face for several seconds. Then they both were enveloped in white light and transported onto the ship. She stood there next to Burrus in shock. Standing before her was Arbiter, Tommy, Fox, and Gunther piloting the ship from the cockpit.

The End turned white as a ghost and she ran over to Fox and Tommy. She wrapped her arms around them and held them close to her, and couldn't contain her cries of relief. "You're alive!" she called out again and again.

"Yes, we are alive," Tommy said with concern in his voice. "Did you think we were dead?"

"Yes," The End released them and tried to wipe her tears away. "I'm sorry; they told me you were dead. They said you two were in the other chairs and that I...fucking executed you this morning."

Fox said, "Those unbelievable bastards. I'm sorry E."

Arbiter piped up, "I was going to say I can't believe they told you that, but they are liars to their rotten cores so I believe it." He smiled and said, "The two people you executed were just filthy atheists like me."

The End smiled and said, "They said they were coming for you too, Arbiter."

"They tried to," he said. "They sent two ships after me, Tommy and Fox defended me from one. Gunther intercepted the second one and took those damn flatcaps out of the sky. He's a hell of a pilot."

"Yes he is," she said and looked up at the pilot. "Gunther!" she called out. "They said you ratted us out!"

The pilot gave a thumbs down.

"It feels so good to be back with you guys," The End said and turned towards Burrus and met his gaze. "Thank you for rescuing me. I had given up...on everything."

Burrus' eyes lit up and he smiled. "I aim to please," he said.

She turned back towards Arbiter and said, "What are we going to do now? I'm sure they revoked my clearance level, so we can't follow our original plan."

"They did," he replied, "but I've already made a dozen other profiles in their database with top level clearance too. I've been demoting people, moving funds around, dispatching troops to the middle of nowhere, listing government property for sale, all kinds of things. It's been so fun, I can't thank you enough for giving me access."

"So we can still distribute the data?" Fox asked.

"Yep, we are good to go. But like I told you, we can't do it remotely. We have to do it from the station on the Justice Floor. It's the only way to broadcast that much data to that many devices in a timely manner. Plus," he turned toward The End, "It will give you a chance to tell everyone the truth."

"Me?" The End said. "I'm not sure what I would say."

"You gotta say something," Tommy said, "people will listen to you before they'll listen to any of us."

Through the rain-streaked window, she spotted her own face on a tall street screen they were passing by. Scrolling text said she was now a criminal against the UO, and that anyone with information must come forward or be executed. Then the image changed to Fox's face with the same message.

"You guys are wanted by the Order too?" The End asked with concern in her voice.

Fox said, "They came for Arbiter. We had to kill them. Corrupt bastards." Her bottom lip started shaking and she continued, "There is no turning back any more. We killed UO officers. We are with you until this is finished."

The End nodded. "Gunther! Take us somewhere we can lay low for a bit."

"I'll head to Nova Scotia," he said. "Arbiter's cabin is the only place where they can't track us."

They quietly flew back to the snowy island and arrived in about fifteen minutes. Gunther set the ship down in the sticky, brown colored snow next to the cabin. They all went inside and Arbiter started a fire in the wood burning stove. The End removed her dented breastplate and laid on the couch. She rolled up her skintight under layer and saw her wounded side. The cut had stopped bleeding but it needed to be cleaned. Fox washed her side with soap and water and wrapped it in gauze bandaging. The End laid in the flickering light from the fire and rested.

Arbiter sat on a chair adjacent to her, Fox was in the kitchen cleaning up the mess, and Gunther was still wearing his flight helmet, leaning against the wall next to the front door with his arms crossed. Burrus stood in the corner of the dining area with a bundle of cords hanging out from the back of his head. His eyes were closed as he relaxed and charged. Tommy sat at the dining table next to him, scraping the last of a portion of baked beans off of his plate.

Arbiter squinted his eyes at The End and said, "E, I have to talk to you about something. It isn't going to be easy."

The End sat up and faced him. "What do you mean?"

"I need you to go to sleep now," he hesitated. "Cede ad somnum."

The End's eyelids fell closed and she became perfectly still.

Tommy stood up from the table and walked over to them frantically, and his voice boomed, "What the hell did you just do to her?"

"I put her to sleep," he said while turning to face The End. He reached toward her and tapped the tip of his finger against her forehead a few times. She remained completely motionless.

Tommy drew his sidearm and aimed the pistol at him. "What the fuck are you playing at? Wake her up."

Arbiter ignored his threat. "I found something when digging around in the UO data stacks. A code phrase to offline her. Temporarily. She won't be harmed."

Fox rounded the corner of the kitchen countertop to cover the other side of the couch. Tommy lowered his side arm to a forty-five degree angle. "Well why did you do it?" he asked.

"I just want to talk. We have to do something."

"About what?" he said.

"About her. She isn't alright. If we attack, they'll stop her."

"Stop her, how?" Fox said and crossed her arms.

"If any of them know that code phrase, which I guarantee someone at the Capitol does, she's toast. If she is taken out of the equation, we will fail. UO will kill us all."

"So what, you want to reprogram her?" Fox said accusingly.

"I want to set her free. Let her make up her own mind for once in her life."

"She already is free, jackoff."

"They sure made it convincing, didn't they? I found a signal within her code. Her mind has a limiter on it. If she thinks certain thoughts –holds certain views about UO –those views are slowly erased from her psyche, and gradually she returns to being their obedient servant again," Arbiter said. "There's more. They were blocking certain memories. One in particular that you all were a part of. When she was relieved from the Future War."

"I'm just supposed to take your word on this?" Tommy asked.

"The only way is to ask her. I could show you the data, but I know you aren't much of a programmer."

"Fuck you."

Burrus walked up behind Tommy and towered over him as he said, "Are you sure you wouldn't rather take a seat?"

Tommy glanced over his shoulder and saw the robot hulking behind him, shook his head, holstered his weapon, and sat on a chair beside Arbiter.

Arbiter turned to look Tommy in the eyes. "Look, I've already removed the restrictions from her code. I just have to plug in this drive to give her a clean boot." He held up the small chip in his hand. "She'll remember everything, and the signal will be blocked. I'll power her on and explain it to her. Either that, or you can deal with Burrus. We are too close to succeeding. I won't let any of you ruin it."

He glanced at Fox and over at Gunther who hadn't moved. "Any thoughts from either of you?"

"Fuck it. Do it," Fox said, "but if you change her in any other way, you'll pay for it. I promise."

Gunther nodded.

"So glad we're in agreement," he said while lifting the blonde hair covering her ear and plugging the drive into a hidden slot in her slender neck. A red light on the small silver drive flashed rapidly after a few seconds, then went dark.

"That's it, all done. I just hope she doesn't kill me." Arbiter said and pushed his glasses up the bridge of his nose. "The End. Surgit."

She suddenly moved her head slightly to the side, blinked rapidly, and looked around the room with a puzzled expression. "What the hell? What happened?" she said and touched her temples with both hands.

"He powered you down, E," Tommy said.

"Powered me down? What are you talking about?" The orange light from the fire danced across her perfectly sculpted face.

Tommy walked over to The End and put his huge hands on her shoulders.

"You okay? How do you feel?" he asked.

She looked down and shifted her glance back and forth as if searching for a long-lost memory. "I feel fine. My mind feels...sharper, I guess. What happened?"

Tommy stepped back and said, "Look, just tell me if you remember the Future War. Do you remember why you left?"

She clasped her hand over her mouth and her eyes flashed open. She let her arm fall to her side and said, "I remember...you all were there. I was taking cover behind a lorry that was tipped over when...a bombardment hit me dead on. I crawled out of the crater with my hands...I felt lighter. When I climbed to the top I rolled onto my back, looked down and...there was just bent metal and severed wires. The shell had blown my lower half to hell. I started screaming and then you-" She looked up at Tommy. "You knelt next to me and you said that I would be alright. You picked me up and carried me away."

Fox wiped her eyes and said, "That was the last time we saw you, E. They took you back, fixed you up. After that, you joined the administration as their executioner."

The End turned toward the pilot and said, "You know about this too?"

Gunther cleared his throat and said, "They told us they were going to block what happened from your memory. And if we spoke to you again," he motioned to slit his throat with his thumb.

Arbiter said, "That's not the only thing UO was keeping from you. Look at this code," he said and spun his laptop around to face her. "I found it when I was snooping around in their files. They've been blocking your thoughts, your actions, and your memories. When I took you offline, I installed a subroutine to delete all of this code from your core systems, and to stop anything else like it from getting installed again."

The End looked astonished and shook her head back and forth. "I can feel it. It's like I had heavy stones rolling around in my head and now they're gone." she glanced over at Arbiter and asked, "But...my father?"

Arbiter shook his head. "He had a hand in your design but technically you don't have parents. From the look of it, he was mainly in charge of shaping your mind to be that of the perfect soldier and eventually, the perfect executioner."

She slammed her fist straight down into the floor, splintering one of the enormous logs that made up the cabin floor. Pieces of wood scattered all around the room and dust filled the air. Two cracks ran up the walls on either side, extending up to the ceiling.

Arbiter waved his hand in front of his face and said, "I forgot to mention, they had some limits on your physical capabilities too, to make you seem more human, probably."

"Woah," she said as she inspected her fist, amazed by her new-found strength.

Arbiter gestured at the floor and said, "But don't worry about this damage, I can get that fixed. I know a guy that fixes completely wrecked houses, it's no problem."

"This place is a shithole," Fox said.

"Let's try one more thing," Arbiter said and sat up straight. "Think back on all of the executions you've done. When you think of them, and recall those memories, what do you feel?"

She saw each execution in chronological order, stored perfectly within her memory. She pictured the little girl, the first child she had executed years ago. The girl was accused of delivering packages to informants for her parents who were branded as terrorists. The End fell to her knees, sank to the floor, and buried her head in her hands and wept.

Arbiter bent down next to her and said, "I'm so sorry. I didn't mean to do that, I just needed to know if you felt what you did was morally wrong. You were being controlled, E. You're not any longer. Don't hate yourself – hate them."

She climbed to her feet and grabbed him by his shirt. "Are you the one trying to control me now? For all I know, you just uploaded something to fuck with my head, to make me side with you and start a rebellion."

"You can check the code yourself. All I did was remove their shackles," he said cautiously. "I'm not asking you to kill anyone, like they have countless times."

"He's got a point, E," Fox said.

She acquiesced and released him. She reached down and grabbed her breastplate from the floor. "Gunther, prep the ship. We're going to the Capitol Building. I'm burning it down."

The pilot gave a thumbs up, turned and walked into the night. The End followed him outside. Arbiter clasped his hands together and said "Well I think that went well, don't you?" and smiled at Fox. Fox rolled her eyes and brushed past him.

When the ship was airborne, The End went into the rear cabin and washed herself. It felt like she was washing her entire past from her. The blood of her patients, the blood from her wounds, and the feeling of the prison cell she was trapped in. Her mind opened and blossomed like a flower as she considered the world for what felt like the first time. She wasn't sure her thoughts or her crushing feelings of remorse were real, but she decided since they were all she had, they were valid enough to be acted upon. She didn't feel empty, she felt alive and coursing with energy and the invigorating need for revenge.

Afterwards, she was still shaken, but was able to put on a fresh suit of her armor once again. She made her hair and makeup look somewhat presentable. She was on edge thinking about how this would be her most watched show ever. She only made one change to her appearance. Instead of a purple stripe across her eyes, she made it bright red. In her mind, she imagined it symbolized the blood of her innocent victims, and the blood that she still needed to spill.

She walked out of the cabin and looked at her teammates.

"This is it. It's time we finish this," she said.

"I agree that people deserve to be punished," Tommy said. "But are you really going to dethrone the leader of the world? You know the chaos it will cause. We could just walk away."

"We can't let this continue," The End said. "I'm beyond saving, for the things that I've done and the things I'm going to do." She extended her hand towards the window of the aircraft, "But this isn't living. This is a world of oppression and imbalance, controlled by avarice and parasites. To have one's freedoms kept buried in the dirt, working for a meager pittance until one has been whittled down so much the only thing they have control over is their own death...it's not an existence worth living."

She paused for a moment and took a deep breath. "Whatever happens after we do this, it will lead to a better world. At the very least, it will be a world with truth. I ask each of you, come with me, and fight along my side. Help me topple the tyrants and break the chains that contain this world. Help the people rise up and create a new future of their choosing. They will spring forth from the ashes towards prosperity, instead of wallowing forever in this filthy sinkhole, fighting to keep things the same. It ends now, with us!'

Everyone called out and cheered at her words, and she smiled at her friends. "Good, then let's move. Gunther, how close are we?"

Gunther said, "One minute out."

"Gunther, when we are in there, take down any ships trying to land or drop off more troops," she replied.

The pilot gave a thumbs up.

The End pointed at Burrus. "You stay with Arbiter and make sure he lives long enough to get the data distributed."

Burrus smiled and nodded in agreement.

Arbiter said "I have a nice little highlight reel from the data that I threw together. We can play it to everyone watching while the data is distributed to their citizen devices."

"Sounds good. Fox, I want you perched with a clear view of the Justice Floor. I want you to have eyes on the Anointed One the whole time, got it?"

Her eyes lit up, "You mean I get to kill that son of a bitch?"

The End smiled and said, "If he tries to escape, put him down." She turned towards Tommy. "You have to make sure we don't get any uninvited visitors during our presentation. Fox will help."

Tommy nodded, "I'm with you E." He opened a weapon locker against the wall and grabbed a new modified Thompson gun, just like his previous one. He ejected the drum magazine, eyed the plasma rounds coiled inside it, then slammed the drum back into the body to load it.

She put her hand on his broad shoulder and smiled, "Thanks, Tommy."

He looked at her and felt his cheeks flush.

Fox marked the building on the north side of the Capitol Building on the holographic map displayed on the gaming table. "I'll be watching from here," she said and walked over to the teleportation pad, then vanished into the light.

Gunther spoke up, "They have security systems up. Incoming teleports are restricted. You'll have to jump."

"That complicates things," The End said. She walked over to the holographic map of the Capitol Building and zoomed in to see each floor. "The Justice Floor is on the 95th, five floors from the top. Can we just drop on the roof?"

"Probably the best bet," Arbiter said. "Burrus can go straight down through the floor so we don't need to worry about fighting through stairs or getting caught up in an elevator."

"But look," Tommy said as he zoomed in on the rooftop. "Lots of guards up here."

"I'll take care of them," Fox said over the comms. Immediately the red outlines of the guards began to disappear as she started hitting them with the flashlight.

"We are straight over the roof. Drop now!" Gunther said as the side door slid open. Arbiter climbed on Burrus' back and jumped first, Tommy and The End followed. They dropped fifty feet down onto Heaven's Reach. There were bodies everywhere around them, still and quiet in the falling rain.

Gunther pulled away just as he started taking fire from two other approaching gunships. He engaged one and peppered it with the chain guns positioned on the aircraft's wings. It pulled away and disengaged. The other gunship was pulling around to line up fire on Gunther. Burrus unleashed a rocket from his shoulder launcher. The missile spiraled toward the ship and entered into its hull. An instant later the ship disintegrated into a massive explosion that shattered the windows of the buildings surrounding them.

"I think they know we're here!" Tommy shouted.

"Burrus! Take us down!" The End called out over a crack of thunder from the clouds surrounding the building top.

The robot nodded and dug his great arms into the gravel floor beneath them, then started shimmying them open to create a hole.

While they watched him, War trotted over to The End and stared at her with its haunting yellow eyes.

"What the hell," Arbiter said. "That scared the hell out of me, these things are so creepy."

"They're just simple robots, nothing to worry about," she said and placed her hand on the top of the metal horse's head between its eyes.

"Should we destroy them?" Tommy asked while aiming his gun at the one with green eyes called Pestilence that was trotting in a wide circle around them.

"No," she said firmly. "I like them. Especially this one."

"You're the boss," Tommy said.

Burrus had worked the hole into a large enough opening for himself and swung into it. The others followed him through and climbed down. The sounds of the storm were suddenly muffled as they found themselves in the grand quarters of the Anointed One; the top floor of the Capitol Building.

Everything was coated in gold, and designed in the most over-the-top fashion imaginable. Lining the walls were extravagant cases full of jewels, diamonds, gold coins, and baubles of all kinds. He even had a golden statue of himself, which The End promptly cut in half diagonally with Ker. The top half crashed to the floor and melted gold flowed down it like blood.

"So this is where all the money's at," Tommy said. "Plenty of neighborhoods could use some of this, that's for sure."

"Get me off this floor, Burrus. This is pathetic," The End said.

Burrus made another hole as Arbiter took some gold coins and quickly lined his pockets. They all jumped down through the new opening to the lower level. The new level was more of the same. Everything was made of gold and filled with treasures from all over the world. They dug down again, and the next two floors were nothing but hoarded trinkets the Anointed One was storing. Rooms full of paintings and statues, taxidermied extinct animals, stolen technology, even antique firearms.

"Why hoard all of this only for it to sit behind locked doors?" The End asked. "I don't get it."

"Some people have to overcompensate," Arbiter said. "The Anointed One has a lot to make up for."

As they rounded a corner, they saw a large room with bright fluorescent lighting along the ceiling. There were rows and rows of tables stacked with packages, and one wall was lined with chemistry apparatuses of all sorts and giant mechanical mixers. They spotted some workers that were packaging bags full of what looked like yellow sand. A head scientist stood at the front of the rows at a computer.

She turned around and spoke loudly to the workers, "Everyone, we have received word that the building needs to be evacuated. Intruders have entered and we aren't sure–" she trailed off upon seeing The End approaching her. "Oh, shit!" she yelled as The End grabbed her by her white coat and lifted her off the ground. The workers ran out of the exits.

"Got a little drug op running here?" The End asked her.

"No, no! We're just storing all the confiscated drugs!" she cried out, her brown curls bouncing across her glasses as she struggled to break from her grasp.

Tommy said, "Bullshit. You know how many drug dens we've raided? We know you're cooking it here, and shipping it out in these boxes.

The End said, "This is the biggest operation I've ever heard of. UO is actually distributing it?"

Tommy walked over and grabbed the scientist's wrist, then held her hand over the rifle of his submachine gun so she had to grab onto it. "You wouldn't lie to us now. A chemist can't do much without her hand."

The scientist looked at him with terror in her eyes and struggled to speak, "Yes, it was McMillan's idea! It's part of his cleansing protocol."

The End set her down but Tommy kept his grip around her wrist. "Keep talking!" he said.

"The General proposed the creation of this drug, so-called 'gold dust'. It was to contain highly-addictive and toxic properties, sterilizing the user immediately and greatly reducing repeated user's brain function. He believed that anyone who used the drug was not worthy of our path forward. This facility has been distributing it for the last twenty years."

Tommy squeezed the trigger and pink plasma rounds tore through the back of the scientist's hand, quickly melting it off at the wrist. He let her go and she screamed in pain and rolled onto her back.

"Let me tell you something," Tommy said. "Both of my brothers died of overdoses from this shit. You can never be forgiven for what you've done here."

The scientist sat up, clutching her wrist with her good hand. She had mascara running down her cheeks and was gritting her teeth in pain. "Good! They were probably human trash. To be stupid enough to take this drug...they are scum and I'm glad they–" Tommy fired rapidly into her body, she slumped over and her clothes set alight.

He turned toward the rows of boxes and opened fire. The rounds cut through the boxes and the flames grew outward from each one. He aimed at the side wall and dumped hundreds of the white-hot plasma rounds into the machinery they were using to cook with. One of the enormous metal mixers exploded, spreading fire in every direction.

"This place is done for, let's go," The End said and put her hand on his shoulder, then walked out of the room into the hallway. He wiped his face on his shoulder and followed her out.

They continued down a long hallway and through a double door. They entered at the top of two curved grand staircases, leading down into an extravagant room below them. They walked down the stairs and spotted someone standing in the room facing them. It was a man standing with his arms straight out from his side making a cross, and he wore no clothing.

The End recognized him immediately. It was the Anointed One. She approached him cautiously and noticed that he had nothing between his legs, like a fake plastic doll. When she circled around to his backside, the skin had been pulled open, revealing a sectioned metal spinal column with thousands of wires sprouting from it. Small gears could be seen within his flayed back, but they were all motionless. The back of his head had been opened, revealing processing units and an internal motherboard.

"Fascinating," Burrus said.

"Jesus," Tommy said. "The Anointed One is a goddamn robot too."

"Why isn't it down on the Justice Floor watching the show?" Arbiter said.

"Fox," The End said. "Do you know where the Anointed One is?"

"Did you guys start a fire?" Fox asked.

"Yeah. The top floors are toast, we'll have to find another way down."

"Copy. I have eyes on him. He's in the balcony seat, chuckling his head off," Fox replied over the comm channel.

"Is he showing up on thermal?" The End asked.

"Let me switch over to it," Fox said. "What the hell? He's an icicle, E."

"So that one's a robot too."

"Well, now I've seen everything. Should I...destroy it?"

"Hold off on that, we can use it to our advantage once we distribute the data."

"Standing by," Fox said.

"There's more than one of them?" Tommy asked.

"Looks like it," The End said and walked through a connecting doorway into the adjacent room. There were a dozen more Anointed Bots standing in the same pose.

"A lot more of them," The End said.

Each of them had balding blonde hair, the same flabby skin hanging from their bloated sides, and double chins that felt real to the touch. The details were incredible, from the varicose veins to the scraggly ear hairs. They even smelled like an unshowered person, the same smell she had noticed on the Anointed One when she was unfortunate enough to be close to him.

The End cleared her throat and said, "Burrus, destroy them all."

The robot nodded. The sounds of metallic destruction filled the air as Burrus began crushing and mangling all of their bodies into scattered pieces. The End walked out into the original room with the robot with its back opened up. Arbiter had plugged into its head with his device.

"How advanced are they?" The End asked.

"Primitive, compared to you," Arbiter said. "It isn't an AI, it just runs the same scripts every day with slight variation, kind of like those horses. Makes sense considering the Anointed One does fuck-all every day. Its first day of operation was timestamped over twenty five years ago. Approved by General McMillan...signed off as a biological replacement."

"Wait, so the original Anointed One is dead?"

"You didn't believe he was actually immortal did you? He died decades ago, and McMillan kept him in power by having these machines stand in his place."

Tommy said, "E, the General has been the one in power the whole time. He was pulling all the strings. The Anointed Bot was just a tool."

"So was The End," a voice came from the hallway outside. The General was dressed in green military dress with his various medals pinned to his chest. He walked towards them, with his arm around a young girl walking next to him. She looked about eight years old, had long blonde hair and wore a white dress with a puffy tulle skirt. The tall, thin man held up a remote in his long, boney fingers and pointed it toward the entrance to the other room and pressed a button. A metal blast door slammed shut, sealing Burrus in the other room.

"Do you know who this is?" the General said with a twisted smile.

The End looked at the small girl and recognized her face from years before, the same face she used to see looking back at her in the mirror. "That's me," she said. "What the fuck is this?"

"Very good," he said and looked down at the girl. "Say hello, my dear."

"Hello," her small voice barely carried through the room. "It's nice to meet you. What's your name?"

"Shut up," she said hesitantly.

"I thought I taught you manners," McMillan said. "Tell your friends to stand down. There is no need for more violence. We can talk to your old self. It will help you remember what you used to stand for."

The little girl smiled and said, "I can tell you about Mastro Titta! Father told me all about him. He says one day I'll be an executioner too."

The End shook her head. "Brainwashing it already, I see. Why did you keep it?" she asked, trying to suppress her anger.

"We made so many of you. We had to give you the illusion of aging, transferring you into bigger and bigger bodies. I kept this one. She listens to everything I say without hesitation. I liked you better that way. Now, come with me," he said and held out his hand.

"Come on, it'll be fun!" The little girl said excitedly.

The End activated her ax and said, "I'll just kill you both and be done with this."

"Before she kills you," Arbiter said. "The Articles of Ascension. The alien artifacts. Where did they come from? The aluminum-lead alloy they're made of can't be created on Earth. How did you get your hands on some?"

"I'm glad to know that we buried the paper trail so well that you don't know the answer to that question, as simple as it is to figure out," The General said. "It's true that aluminum-lead alloys can only form while in a zero-gravity environment. In a gravity field, the lead and aluminum will always separate. But humans had been in space for sixty years at that point. We forged it ourselves, brought it back to Earth, and rewrote the rules of the new world upon it."

"So it was metal from space, but aliens didn't make it," Tommy said.

"Of course not, you dolt," the General said while narrowing his eyes.

"How could you be okay with willingly causing that much chaos?" The End said. "You're a monster."

"I tested our species, that is all," he snapped. "I asked us all if we were worthy to live as one species. We have failed the test. I thought humanity was smarter than it turned out to be. I didn't realize that half the planet would rather resist the necessary future. Force us to destroy our world rather than live in coexistence with one another. Now there are so few resources to go around I have to come up with new ways to...cull the weak, so the strong may persist."

"Coexistence? That's what you call being forced to change religions and give up all of your freedoms? To know that you're the one behind the gold-dust crisis to–"

"Drugs have plagued us since the dawn of civilization. I'm only trying to keep an addict's genes out of the pool. You know we'd be better off without them."

"I've had enough of your half-assed justifications. You're insane to think that anyone deserves that much control over other people."

"That's fine, we don't have to talk here. I'll just have to take you with me and install new, more robust restrictions. After my associates kill your friends, that is." He gestured to the doorway behind him as two massive robots walked through it on all four limbs, exactly how Burrus walked. They had the same glowing red face screens, and halted behind the General.

"Shit, two of them survived," Arbiter said while dragging his hand down his face.

McMillan stared at The End and said, "Time to rest now, my dear. Cede ad somnum."

Upon uttering the code phrase, The End's eyes closed shut, her body slumped over, but she remained standing. Ker fell to the ground and deactivated. General McMillan walked towards her and said, "Stand back," to Tommy and Arbiter. He pulled her crimson hood back, then ran his fingers through her long, blonde hair, tucking the strands behind her ear. "You're always causing so much trouble," he said quietly to her as he lifted a data drive up to plug into the slot behind her ear.

She opened her eyes and looked at him. Just as he realized she had been pretending, she gripped his throat with her hand.

"Sorry to disappoint you, father."

His eyes bulged as she closed her fist shut, ripping his throat completely out and tossing the marred gore to the ground. He stumbled backwards and clutched at the gaping wound. His face turned white as the blood drained from it and dyed his uniform red. He fell to the ground and started thrashing around in his own blood, helplessly making strained gurgling sounds.

The End bent down, picked up her ax, activated it and held it in front of her with both hands. Arbiter stepped back and took cover behind a large metal desk in the corner. Tommy shouldered his gun and opened fire on one of the enemy gorillas. It shielded itself with its broad forearms, but he kept it at bay. The End ran and slid toward the other one and tried to do an upward slashing strike from below. It jumped out of the way and did a somersault through the air, landing behind her. It grabbed her by the head and tossed her across the room, caving the wall in with the force of the impact.

"What's going on?" Fox shouted across the comms. "I can't see anything!"

Arbiter dove forward next to the General's corpse and pried the small remote control from his fingers. He pressed a button and the blast doors opened. Burrus thundered into the room and tackled the robot Tommy was shooting at. They tumbled across the floor, just past the little girl who was still standing perfectly still. They crashed through tables filled with piles of research papers and computer stations, then slammed into bookshelves against the wall. Burrus landed on top, pinning the other ape on its back. He shifted his knees atop the robot's upper arms, then pressed his fingers under its jaw and pulled upwards, denting the metal and straining until the bolts broke and the robot's head came off.

The End was on her feet again and ran toward the other robot. She drew back a baseball swing and unleashed it toward its torso with all her strength. The ape clapped his enormous hands together on the ax head, catching it perfectly and stopping it. It tried to pull the weapon away from her but she broadened her stance and gripped the staff as hard as she could, fighting against its immense strength with her own.

Burrus stood over the headless machine, holding his victim's head in his right hand. He raised it into the air then smashed the head into the still metal body again and again, as oil and bolts sprayed across the room with every new rupture. Still the girl stood motionless, her small head turning from one fight to the other, watching curiously as the black oil drops stained her pristine dress.

Tommy aimed his gun at the ape that was locked in a stand-off with The End. Arbiter put his hand on his gun and lowered it. "Wait," he said and pointed the remote toward the ape. He pressed another button and the red glowing face powered down. It released its grip on The End's ax and stood straight up with its arms hanging at its sides.

"You shut it down?" she said while glancing back at Arbiter.

"Now we have two of them," he said and smiled under his bushy gray beard.

The End sheathed Ker and walked over to the little girl. Burrus walked up behind her.

"Are you okay?" The End asked her.

The girl looked up at her. The End took the fabric of her crimson cloak and wiped a drop of oil from the girl's porcelain cheek. "Let's get you out of here."

The girl blinked her long eyelashes slowly and said, "Mortui sumus," in her small voice.

"Oh no, no, no," Arbiter said. "Burrus, take her!" He yelled as the girl's eyes turned to a bright glowing red. Burrus picked up the girl by the shoulders and turned around, placing himself between the girl and The End when the girl's body exploded. The force knocked everyone to the ground as a giant fireball rose in a plume against the ceiling. The End sat up and looked for Burrus. There was nothing more than a few gnarled pieces of metal where he stood moments before.

"He's gone," The End said somberly. "He saved me."

Arbiter stood up while coughing and fanning smoke with his hands. He saw the destruction and meekly looked for any trace of his friend.

Fox talked in their ears, "What's going on in there?"

"We're okay, Fox," The End said. "Standby."

Arbiter walked over to the debris and put his hands on his hips. "Well, that's a bummer," he said.

The End stood up and said, "Thought you'd be more beat up about this."

"Well, I would be," he said and walked over to the robot he had disabled remotely, which had tipped over from the explosion and now laid on its side. "But–" he tapped on his citizen device furiously. "--just have to give this one a complete data wipe...and upload Burrus' code here...and give it a clean boot."

The robot's screen lit up in bright green and faded to the familiar image of the gorilla's face. The screen showed Burrus open his eyes and smile.

"There we go. Good as new," Arbiter said. The new Burrus climbed to his feet and galloped in a half circle, then skidded to a stop. He looked over at them and said, "Please stay close. Time is short."

"Not so fast, buddy," Arbiter said and walked over to the Anointed Bot that was still standing at the other end of the room. "Destroy this thing."

Burrus ran over and grabbed the Anointed Bot by the head and sheared it in half, scattering screws, gears, and computer parts across the room.

"Splendid. Shall we?" Burrus said.

The End shook her head and said, "Never a dull moment with you two around. Glad you're still with us, Burrus. Thanks for saving me."

He smiled at her. She pulled up a holo map on her device and walked out of the room into the hallway. She led the team to the opposite corner of the level and stopped. "Well, here we are. The

Justice Floor is right under us. Tommy and I can drop through right over the stage. Then Burrus can create another opening for Arbiter to access the studio control room, which is on the South side of the room. Here."

With her order, Burrus smashed both hands down on the ground, creating a small opening. The End dropped down and landed in the center aisle between the audience on the Justice Floor. The audience gasped at the sudden disruption.

The host peered out into the audience and said, "Ladies and gentlemen! It looks like our old executioner has returned. This is most unexpected. Perhaps, she is looking to challenge her replacement?" Tommy clumsily crashed to the ground behind her and she felt her cheeks turn red. "If so," the host continued, "by the rights and laws upholding the tradition of an honorable duel, you'll have to face him alone."

The Cleanser stood with both hands on his hips in a wide stance next to the host. His voice came through the speakers, "By the blessed authority of the Anointed One, you are to be executed here and now, one way or another. Come sit upon this chair, accept your fate, and let's be done with it."

A suit ran up to The End and quickly fastened a mic to her crimson cloak. She ran a cloth over her armor and face to get rid of the oil splatters, whispered, "It's good to have you back", then ran backstage.

"I have not come to challenge you," The End spoke loudly. "I have come to share the truth about the United Order, and show the world what the Anointed One really is!" She pointed towards the leader of the UO, who was sitting in his usual balcony seat, squinting down at her with his hands folded across his large stomach. The two elite guards by his side stood up and brandished their rifles.

"Kill her," he said with pursed lips. One of the two elite guards spoke into a wrist microphone briefly, relaying the order to his troops.

The End rushed toward the stage, activating Ker as she ran. The crowd gasped and cried out as flatcaps poured through the side doors. In the ruckus, the sounds of Burrus and Arbiter crashing into the control room were muffled. Then, the high pitched whine of Tommy's plasma rounds filled the air and they shredded an entire squad of flatcaps from one doorway. The UO soldiers storming through the other entrance opened fire on The End. Rounds loudly ricocheted off of her armor, but as she was running her right arm was hit several times, and a few rounds hit her in the right side, making her fall to the ground. She looked over at her assailants just in time to see them get mowed down by Tommy's spray of fire. More of them kept coming as Tommy pinned them down.

The End lay on the floor cursing and in shock from being hit. The Cleanser ran over to her and raised his sword above his head again, ready for a downward thrust. The End quickly spun Ker around, parrying the strike and staggering him backwards. She hopped up on her feet, but dropped the ax to the ground as blood streamed down her arm and dripped from her fingertips. She quickly bent down and picked it up with her left arm.

"Ah," The Cleanser said. "This will be easy, I have the advantage."

"I can still take you with only one arm. You don't stand a chance. Shut up and fight!"

Suddenly a white flash of light streaked through the room, and one of the elite guards standing next to the Anointed One dropped dead. Then another pierced through the second guard's chest. The Anointed One bulged his eyes out in surprise, and struggled to get up. He noticed Fox's laser sight on his chest and froze in fear.

"There ya go," Fox said over comms. "Now ya get it, dumbass. You're not going anywhere."

As The End watched the balcony, The Cleanser reared back and slashed at her. The blade entered her in a small gap in her chest armor on the right side. The blade's heated light cut straight through her ribs and seared her flesh, making her fall to her knees. She had never felt such crippling pain before. She cried out in agony as he pulled the blade from her and turned to walk away.

With her remaining strength, she gripped Ker and slashed upwards at him in a lightning fast streak of pink light. His leg tumbled away from him, completely severed at his upper thigh. He fell to the ground, grasping at his wound as blood spilled from it into a wide, slowly growing pool atop the black stone of the Justice Floor.

She saw that his sword had fallen and was lying on the ground beside him. She lifted Moros and used it for balance as she stood up. She limped over to him.

"Impossible," he said with a strained voice. "The blade touched your flesh, you should be dead!"

She lifted the black, flickering blade and plunged it downward into his chest. The blade impaled him easily and stuck into the floor beneath him.

"You can't kill something that isn't alive, asshole," she said while staring into his eyes.

He struggled against it for a few moments, before giving into his fate and lying motionless. The End watched him die as she breathed heavily and clutched her side. Blood and oil ran from beneath her chest piece.

"We don't have a lot of time," she said to her team. "Arbiter, what's your status?"

"It's all ready to go, E," he replied. "Waiting on your signal."

"Tommy," she said while pointing at the Anointed One in the balcony seat. "Bring him to me."

Tommy nodded and walked up the side stairs, lifted the Anointed One from his chair and marched him to the front of the stage. The crowd gasped and some people cried out in fear of what would happen to their beloved leader. The suit that fastened her microphone to her armor approached The End and wiped the blood from her armor with a towel.

"Are you okay to do this?" she asked. "You're in pretty bad shape."

"I'm not worried about what happens to me," The End replied. "I'm worried about what will happen if I don't succeed."

"Well, I took it to commercial once the flatcaps stormed in. We are about to go live again, I'll give you the signal," she said while motioning to the control room. Burrus and Arbiter were inside looking back at her. Burrus gave her a thumbs up, and she gave one back with her good arm. "Thank you," she said to the suit.

She went back to her station outside the control room, and counted down with her fingers; 3...2...1...live.

"Fellow citizens of the United Order of America. My name is The End. I am the former head executioner for the order. I'm speaking to you all because I've found information critical to our survival. Things can't go on like this. I believe that in order for humanity to persevere we need to hold truth above all else; reason, understanding, and truth are the core to our success as a species. The world that we have been unfortunate enough to find ourselves in doesn't respect these values. We have all been living under a veil of lies. The biggest of them all is that our leader is not a leader at all—" she activated Ker, "—but a clever deception. Observe."

She stepped back and slashed him at the shoulder. His arm came off easily, and he had no reaction. The crowd began screaming out in a panic as The End bent down and picked up the arm. She held it in front of her so the audience could see and the cameras could get in a close shot. There was some blood, but no bone or tendons or flesh as they expected. She crushed it with her hands and ripped it apart and showed the audience the metal joints, wiring, bolts, and grease. The crowd calmed as they slowly realized it wasn't a real person.

"This is not a man, it is a machine – a puppet this administration used to fool us all into thinking this man was immortal!" The End announced. "After uncovering this, I brought the people who were responsible to justice, as I am sworn to do. If you need further proof of the lies of this government, I invite you to take a look at the data we have found. This data shows that the Enlightened One himself was also a robotic machine, just like this one, used to give ultimate political control to the Anointed One."

The audience gasped, their voices raising in protest. She stepped aside as the video played, showing the audience and the world an edited version of the same footage they had seen earlier. The audience wept and cried out in sadness over the senselessness of it all.

"These raw files are being distributed permanently to your citizen device for each and every citizen to review at their discretion." She walked over to the shiny metal tablets displayed upon stage. She activated Ker and held it up to the engraved lettering. "These articles were not written on an alloy brought from alien beings, they were created by this administration as well. I hereby erase the Articles of Ascension." She dragged the hot blade down each line of the text and the words transformed into molten metal, pooling at the bottom of the stand. When the faces of each tablet was blank, she deactivated her ax and holstered it.

She turned to address the audience again, "I felt that it was extremely important—" she became light-headed and stumbled backwards a step, cleared her throat and continued, "Everyone needed to know. But as all of you also know, I have been a main contributing factor in this administration being able to get away with all of this. I have killed thousands of innocent people, allowing this lie to perpetuate. If this world is to be rebuilt, all who were involved in this corruption must be erased. I am beyond redemption, but I will do one final act of justice to try to make up for the darkness I have bred." She grabbed onto the Anointed One, who was still motionless and facing forward, and slowly began backing towards the window. She slipped on her own blood that had pooled at the base of her boots, but caught herself on the broad shoulders of the Anointed Bot.

As they walked toward the window, the audience cried out in protest. Some detested her decision, others called her traitorous and called for her death. They rose to their feet and shouted at her, their voices blending together into an incoherent jumble of noise.

Tears welled in the Arbiter's eyes as The End reached the windowed wall. He grabbed onto Burrus, who also had tears in his artificial eyes. Tommy shook his head and lowered his gaze to look at the floor. Fox watched from the adjacent rooftop as the Anointed One was thrown out of the window of the 95th floor, and The End leapt out after him. They both fell for an eternity, completely at the mercy of gravity and silhouetted by blue and orange flashes of firebolts stretching across the clouds. Gunther saw them falling and frantically keyed into the teleporter pad, but she was moving too quickly to be transported.

In the elevated plaza, far below at the foot of the tower, The End's broadcast caused a crowd to form. They witnessed both falling bodies impact the ground in front of them. The two robots exploded into mechanical parts as the onlookers cheered.

Two years later, the sun shone brightly onto the Capitol Building. Flags from many re-established countries were raised proudly to show unity against the tyranny that previously corrupted the world. In the patches of billowing clouds above the city, swarms of drones flew within them, tasked with filtering toxins out of the atmosphere. People were gathered again to partake in the annual celebration of the revolution.

At the entrance of the Capitol Building, a statue was displayed. It was not a statue of bronze or stone, but of meticulously reassembled metal parts from their bodies that had been reconstructed and posed. The hero sat mounted on the metal horse, War, with one hand pointing forward and toward the sky. The other hand was gripping Ker, with the head of the famed ax balanced on her shoulder. Cast at the feet of the horse was her felled foe: the Anointed One, who was burst open and fatally wounded.

A little girl walked with her mother through the gathering of people who were dancing and singing together. She let go of her mother's hand and ran over to a statue. The little girl stared up at the statue wide-eyed as her mother joined her.

"Who is that, mommy?" the little girl asked.

The mother smiled and said. "That's the one who saved us all. Her name was The End."

ACKNOWLEDGEMENTS

Thanks to the creative writing community at Colorado State University for helping to elevate my work in a myriad of ways. Thanks to Prof. Lynn Badia for teaching me that fiction should be weird and unsettling. Thanks to Prof. Dana Masden for teaching me invaluable lessons and taking the time to help me refine these stories. Thanks to Prof. Mike Smith, head of Astronomy at FRCC, for opening my mind to the intricacies of the universe and for making sure the science in my writing was sound. Thanks to my parents for giving me a life full of experiences and for choosing Colorado. Special thanks to Kellen Tomcak for reading through everything I've ever written and for always being honest in his critiques. Special thanks to Maddie Gudenkauf for believing in my work and taking this leap into publication with me. Thanks most of all to my lovely wife, Megan, for showing me how amazing and beautiful life can be. You are my inspiration and I couldn't have achieved this without you.

Edgar Paul Hubbs is a fiction writer, debuting his anthology: *Paradigm and Other Short Stories*. Growing up in Colorado, he enjoyed the hiking trails and ski resorts of the Rocky Mountains. Space has always fascinated him and he loves to study the cosmos with his telescope. He is an alum of Colorado State University. He lives in Northern Colorado with his wife Megan and their two dogs.

Follow the Author:
www.ephubbs.com
Twitter: @EPHubbs

Please Review It!

Reviews are essential to indie authors and small publishers. They allow new readers to discover the book and, depending on the platform, increase the likelihood of the book appearing elsewhere on the site. So if you really enjoyed this novel and want others to read it, it would be appreciated if you reviewed it on your platform of choice!

Thank you!!

www.dalygoodmedia.com
dalygoodbusiness@gmail.com

www.ingramcontent.com/pod-product-compliance
Lightning Source LLC
Chambersburg PA
CBHW070509300726

48975CB00007B/2379